THE MIGHTY OAK

THE MIGHTY OAK

JEFF W. BENS

**BLACK
STONE**
PUBLISHING

Printed in the United States of America

First edition: 2020
ISBN 978-1-982604-16-5
Fiction / General

1 3 5 7 9 10 8 6 4 2

CIP data for this book is available
from the Library of Congress

Blackstone Publishing
31 Mistletoe Rd.
Ashland, OR 97520

www.BlackstonePublishing.com

For my mother, Meg Bens

And we are put on earth a little space,
That we may learn to bear the beams of love.

—William Blake

"Anybody who says they don't like fighting in the
NHL have to be out of their minds."

—Don Cherry

1

When his sister Arlene called from Boston to say their mother was dead, Oak was in an ice bath halfway through a twelve-pack of beer in the middle of the Texas afternoon, trying to concentrate on how he was going to knock Pat McDonald's head in. Outside his apartment, the El Paso sun blazed. Inside, he had the apartment lights off, as he kept them, against the wavering sickness in his head. He hadn't slept again. He hasn't slept much since the headaches that crept in over the summer, his hip and lumbar throbbing in their marrow. His ma wasn't supposed to be dead. When Oak talked to her in July, three months ago, she said she was better, that her cancer was on the run.

Out the team bus window, a cattle truck rattles his head. The El Paso Storm bus rolls north through the Chihuahuan desert on the way to the Albuquerque, New Mexico rink, at the far northern edge of the West Texas Hockey League. Oak sits alone in a seat at the back of the bus with the other veteran players. The boys are playing cards, they're on their phones. The bus smells of sweat, IcyHot, booze breath, and beer farts. Oak takes a drink from the roadie he's got between his knees. He's got a seat reserved on a 4:00 a.m. Greyhound back from Albuquerque to El Paso and a ticket for a flight from El Paso to Logan for tomorrow afternoon. For after he knocks Pat "Sandman" McDonald's head off.

Oak examines his right fist. He locates the first knuckle of his right index finger down near the middle of his palm. He works the knuckle toward the base of his finger, sets it more or less back into place. He's got nothing against Pat McDonald. The Albuquerque defenseman is twenty-two, is making a name for himself. Oak understands this. But he's going to do it, he has to do it, even though McDonald tomahawked Ken Grimes's neck with his stick last spring when Oak wasn't even skating, when Oak was collapsed-out in his shitty El Paso apartment with his spinning head and his stitched-up post-surgery lumbar spine.

He kept meaning to get back to Boston. From Texas. From Florida where he was before Texas. He hasn't seen his daughter Kate. He's ashamed that it will take his own mother's funeral for him to see his daughter, to see Kate for the first time in four years. Kate was ten, and now she is fourteen. Oak was ten. And now he is thirty-two. Oak looks back out the bus window at Texas. The sunlight slashes through the gap between his sunglasses and his face. He squeezes his eyes shut again. He hears the blood ringing in his brain. He just needs ice time. To get out of Texas and back up a league. And then another league, up to where he belongs.

Oak gets the plastic pill bottle from the pocket of his sweats. He needs six Oxy 40s a day to get the job done, with Dexy or Adderall. The team doctor cycles him through Vicodin and Tramadol, with Ativan and Ambien. Oak pays for the Oxy and the Dexedrine.

He's always had headaches but last February they had started to mess up his brain. The pills help. He remembers the game when he first really zeroed out. Two years ago in Florida. Nothing really bad had happened. He hadn't even fought. He took a blindside hit from some goon and then it was an hour later and the game was over. Oak was dressing at his locker when he came to. He's had his bell rung too many times to remember, drifted ten minutes here and there on the bench but he always came to. Drank some water. Head-butted the boards to wake himself back up. But that time, in the Florida locker room, when he woke to see his teammates doing their usual shit, laughing so he knew they must have won the game, he remembers the smell of rotting fruit. And then he fell against the dressing room bench and puked on the carpet, the boys giving him shit like he was hungover. He shoved a smile on his face, getting to the toilet stall where he sat for he can't remember how long, steadying his brain in his busted-up hands.

He spaces the Oxy out, eats them in bursts before games. His soft head led to his busted back. His busted back led to more pills. He knows it. He's read about it. Addiction. CTE. He's not going down that path, over the Mexican border with a Pringles can of pills. But the team doctor and dentist are scaling him back. So he's paying premium. He no longer gives a shit what he looks like in practices—he knows he just needs to get his body back in order, his head straightened out. He doesn't even want to take the shit anymore, but if he doesn't then he can't sleep, can't think, can't skate.

He tries to remember to park his truck at the back right corner of parking lots. He writes down that he's eaten. He puts his keys and his phone on a table that he moved next to his apartment door so he can always remember to take them.

A semi bursts past the bus window. Oak washes the Oxy down with the beer. "We're showmen, Oak," their coach Tom Bowie said to him three weeks ago on opening day when Oak fought his first fight since February, his first of six in this season's first ten games, not counting the punch-up last week in the team bar parking lot that their mouthy Long Island–born winger started and Oak had to finish. "No one wants to see you finessing a wrist shot."

Maybe it's true, he thinks. On opening day there were posters for him, flashing phones. The El Paso Storm crowd chanted his name. *He's baaaack*, the rink PA said, Oak watching himself overhead on the Jumbotron delivering hit after hit, punch after punch: for Texas, before that for Florida, for North Carolina in the ECHL, the crowd and him rising together. He's fifteen and scoring, he's twenty and skating, he's twenty-five and falling, from the AHL to the ECHL, he's thirty-two and closing his eyes behind his shades on a Texas League bus to Albuquerque.

He turns toward the bus window again, twists an Adderall 20 capsule and sucks the Addy up his nose. In his head, he sees pictures: his dead ma smoking at his games when he was a kid, his sister Arlene step-dancing on a St. Paddy's float, his father in a black donkey coat standing by the MBTA trains. And there's Shannon and their baby, Kate, napping in his Providence College hockey house bed. His sister Arlene said Shannon and Kate will be at the funeral on Monday. Kate will be there when they lower his ma into the ground.

THE ALBUQUERQUE RINK IS OLD, steaming with bad air and wet ice. Banners for an MMA fight and a monster truck show hang from the rafters. Oak and his teammates skate on into a fog of boos. The Albuquerque fans pound the glass. They know what's coming. They want it. They've paid for it. Oak skates to the visitor's bench. He shouts over the boards to his coach Tom Bowie, Major Tom. "You gonna let me skate today, Major?"

Major Tom scratches his mustache, spits into the corner of the bench. His coach, his friend. They fished together. They used their sticks on the back nine in the Franklin Mountains, slapping golf balls out toward Juarez. "Just skate your game, Oak," Major yells back, not meeting Oak's eyes.

The rink lights snap off. Oak steadies himself against the spots that swirl the ice. He swallows hard, jams his teeth together. He's sweating good now, with what's in him, with what he is going to do to Pat McDonald. The spots spin across the ice, the PA growling, "Don't Poke the Bull if You Don't Want the Horns!" as the snorting, flag-waving mascot leads the Albuquerque team onto the ice, steam blasting from the mascot's plastic nose, Metallica's "Enter Sandman" shaking the arena's air.

Oak looks for Pat McDonald. The Jumbotron flashes a montage of the Bulls scoring, hitting, and fighting. Oak opens and closes his gloved fists, shifts his weight from one skate to the other. Up above him, McDonald delivers a massive uppercut to some bender's strapless chin, a halo of sweat exploding from the poor guy's hair. The image freezes. The crowd chants "Sandman" as the rink lights burn back on. A coke sails down from the stands, hits Oak, ice and coke running down his back. The Albuquerque crowd bunches near Pat McDonald, waving Sandman posters, snapping photos of McDonald with their phones. In person, Oak realizes, McDonald is even bigger and dumber than he looks online. His head is like a cement block.

Oak sucks in, blows out, pushes off from the boards. He loops behind their net and smacks his forehead against the corner glass. The fans think he's showboating. He does it again. Grinding his mouthpiece, he skates hard small circles in the visitor's end. Later, he tells his body. He punches the boards to wake-up his bleeding fists. He drives his knees into the air. I'm still the boss of you, he's telling his body, he's telling his head, he's telling his sick, throbbing blood.

He roars into speed. His teammates grin, stick-slap him as he goes by, Grimesy nodding, Oak squeezing life from every cell he's got. He skates the center line. One of the Albuquerque guys says something to him, about how he's done, about how he should go fuck his Texas boyfriend. Oak loops harder around their end, he's flying now, and he cuts over the center line just as McDonald loops by. Oak grabs the kid and spins him. He's not waiting on the National Anthem, he's not waiting on the puck. He's peaking, in half an hour his body will start its grinding collapse.

"Let's go," Oak says.

"Later, Pops," McDonald says. One of McDonald's front teeth is gone. Up close, Oak can see the baby fat on the kid's face.

"Now." Oak drops his gloves, hurls his helmet so that it smacks against the boards. For a split second, waiting on McDonald to drop, an unfamiliar thought flashes in the rising white roar inside Oak—that he doesn't have to fight. That he's a dog in a pit. In that flash, Oak lets McDonald's ham fist shoot past his right ear, and Oak straightens the kid with three quick blows—chin, nose, temple. McDonald shove hooks the side of Oak's head, Oak flashing into starburst. The blow is like a thrown brick. The crowd roar white-tunnels into nothing, time slowing, as McDonald tries to hook again, the silence spinning as the benches clear around them. Oak ducks, comes back up. McDonald clenches. Oak's been waiting on this. He studied McDonald's clench online. The kid always leaves a gap. Oak shoots a tight uppercut with his right fist into this gap between their two chests. McDonald's head snaps backward as Oak knew it would. McDonald's head floats there in front of Oak, a fat, dumb balloon. Oak draws the punch from his legs to his waist to his shoulder to his fist and smashes it. McDonald falls silently into the whiteness, the guy's head bouncing off the ice.

Oak times the bounce as the noise and color rush back in. He hurls a roundhouse to the side of McDonald's face, the force of his own punch bringing Oak to his knees. McDonald's head bursts into blood spray. The roundhouse sends McDonald sliding, his bleeding face smearing the ice. McDonald balls up. The fights around them freeze. The ref gets in front of Oak and suddenly the ref starts screaming for the rink doctor. Oak hears his own heart and breath. Cups rain from the stands.

"Oak—"

Major Tom runs across the glove-littered rink.

"Oak—"

Oak sees his mother dead on her white-tiled bathroom floor. He sees his daughter, Kate, skating in white snow.

"Oak—"

There's a doctor in red sweats running behind Major Tom. Oak watches them, the doctor slipping on the ice, racing toward McDonald. McDonald lays motionless. Getting closer, Oak sees McDonald's bloodied face. And then he has to look again against what he thinks he is seeing and it's there: McDonald's right eyeball is hanging wet and red from his shattered eye socket to the blood pool on the ice. The quiet explodes. Two Bulls jump Oak from behind, the blows on him like blocks thrown into black water.

LATER, IN THE PARKING LOT, with the delayed game starting, Oak looks up at the black Albuquerque sky. An ambulance took Mc-Donald away. Oak knew better than to try to see him. Oak just walked up the ramp, and even the fans were quiet, he walked through that quiet and got his skates off and his pads and he showered off the fight, his whole body shaking so that he had to sit down in the stall. He is still shaking in the parking lot, standing there shaking, when three guys come over, having left the game.

"There's kids in there," one guy says.

"You sick bastard."

"You may have killed the guy."

When the biggest guy throws a punch, Oak takes it, to the side of his face, and falling as he takes another punch, he lets the guys take their shots, their punches dissolving in the adrenaline that burns cold inside him. Looking up at the night sky from the Albuquerque parking lot, Oak can feel what they've done to his face and ribs, he can see it in the face of the smallest guy as they run—and he is lying on his back on Castle Island in Southie with his girlfriend Shannon, looking at the Boston stars, Kate still in that place for souls before they get ripped into life.

2

Oak sits in the front seat of his sister Arlene's Voyager in the funeral procession from Our Lady in Southie to the cemetery by the park. Arlene's driving. Her husband Kyle and their two kids are in the back in matching blue suits. Oak hardly knows his nephews, Tommy and Jack. He maybe saw them when he was last home, four summers ago, when he last saw Kate. Kate's going to be at the burial. Slats was at the service in the church. He told him Shannon and Kate would be at the burial. Slats his boyhood best friend who went and married Shannon.

Oak's wearing his shades in the rain like an idiot. He's wearing them against the daylight banging in his head. He spent the plane ride from El Paso to Boston soaking his clothes with sweat. He locked himself in the airplane bathroom, put the seat down, and tried to breathe. His face is fucked up from the Albuquerque parking lot. His ribs. A flight attendant knocked on the door. He didn't know where he was. When he woke this morning in his boyhood bed, he didn't know where he was either.

"And you'll be okay alone tonight at the house, Tim?" Arlene asks. His sister lives in Stoneham, with a lawn and a garage, a half hour away.

"Sure."

"Because last night—"

"I had jet lag on top of, you know, everything." He walked the neighborhood, parked himself on a bench by the water.

"We haven't even talked about how you look."

"You beat guys up, Dad says," the bigger nephew says.

"Jack—" Arlene says.

"I didn't say it like that," her husband Kyle says.

"Only when they deserve it," Oak manages to say.

They drive.

"I didn't even know where to call him." Arlene shakes her head, like it's what they've been talking about.

Oak knows she means their father. "He's not still in Florida?"

"I have no idea, Tim."

"Who?" Tommy asks.

"Your grandpa," Kyle says.

"We never ever met him," Jack says.

"He's not dead," Arlene says quickly. Oak side-glances her. His father took off when Oak was a freshman at PC and Arlene was a junior at Holy Cross. He could be dead.

"Grammy is," the smaller one, Tommy, says.

Oak wants to say something, to be an uncle, to tell them how she loved them both, but he has no idea. At the church service, the boys sat lifeless next to their parents, Arlene gripping Oak's hand. Jim Sharkey was there—Oak's boxing coach, his father's friend. "Come see me, Tim," Shark said at the service, Shark still tall and strong, in his great coat and big glasses, his hands like bricks and his forearms like thick black rope. "I will," Oak said not knowing if it was true. When Oak turns to look at his nephews, his head swimming, he sees Shark through the back window of his sister's Voyager, Shark's gaze steady and unyielding behind the wheel of his car.

"You guys skate?"

The kids look at him. The older one has Arlene's brown oval eyes, the younger one Oak's ma's pointed nose. Oak sees how his own face looks in the uncertainty in their eyes.

"Hey—" Kyle says.

"Yes," the smaller one says, to be polite.

Oak thinks to smile at them, his lips crusted from the parking lot blows. He turns back to face the front. He doesn't want to see Kate. He can't see his daughter with the way he is, beat-down, bruised-up, his hands wrecked, his hip, his spine, with what he did to Pat McDonald on infinite loop in his brain. When he closes his eyes, he sees McDonald's bloodred eyeball looking back at him from the inside of his own closed lids.

"Hey, tim?" and it's later and his cheek is against the car window. When he opens his eyes, he sees gravestones. When Arlene pulls the Voyager to their mother's gravesite, Slats and Shannon and Kate are already there together, standing in the rain beneath a cluster of elms. She's tall now and beautiful, always beautiful, his daughter's face bright even in the sadness and the rain. She's fourteen. Her red hair is streaked with blue.

Oak gets out of his sister's car.

"Ah, man, Oak," Slats says when he sees him again and they hug, Oak looking past Slats's shoulder to Shannon and Kate who see him now, too. Slats is still skinny, his hair cropped, the Holy

Name tattoo on his neck is weathered, like Slats has been working outside. Oak takes his sunglasses off. To give it to Kate all at once.

He sees again how he looks, but this time in Shannon's eyes as he gets there, in the eyes of the mother of his daughter, who slid away from him, when they were younger, who no doubt thinks he slid away from her. Shannon has her hand on Kate's back. Like they are tethered. Their daughter's face goes wide into a surprising smile when Oak joins them. Slats stands behind him. Oak can feel him there. Her cheeks, her blue eyes, her big white teeth squeeze at him and he feels a compression in his chest. He's stuck to the mud. Kate steps forward and hugs him. He gets his arms around his daughter but he doesn't really know if he should be doing it, he rests them there on her back, the look on Shannon's face twining the shame and fear and anger inside of him, the smell of his daughter's hair and neck collapsing time and pulling at his heart's defense.

Kate steps back to look at him. She's as tall as his chin. And then she suddenly starts crying and when he steps toward her she cringes and turns away.

"We'll talk to you after," Shannon says steadily, the first words between them in four years. "She wanted to come."

"I'll come see you," Oak says to Kate's back.

"Why?" his daughter says to the wet tree and then she is leaning her whole body against the trunk, Shannon resting her hand again on their daughter's back, Slats coming over to stand between them. Oak doesn't know what to do. Oak wants to knock Slats to the cemetery grass, if only to give Slats an excuse to get up and knock him back harder. Slats whispers to Kate, about the tree, about her grandmother, about how she doesn't have to do anything she doesn't want to do, Kate wiping her face with her sweater sleeve.

When Oak turns, Shark's already at the gravesite, watching him.

There's a dozen people around his mother's grave: nurses from the old age home where she volunteered cutting hair, some neighbors that he half recognizes. They are standing in the cemetery down by the park where he played street hockey as a kid. An altar boy opens an umbrella over Father Larry Pierce. Larry who Oak's known since Our Lady where they went to school together. Larry who was caught at age twelve at the public pool with his hand down another boy's shorts. Larry the weird kid who was chased down the school halls until Oak got sick of seeing it and threw buck-toothed Tommy Mahoney against a locker and then for good measure slammed Ted Prievis's head into a water fountain when they were all fourteen. Arlene squeezes his hand. Oak looks back at his daughter, a young woman in a sweater and a skirt. He looks at her blue eyes that are Shannon's, at her smile that is his ma's and sort of even a better version of his. Slats holds Kate's hand. Oak turns back to the dirt, the shame in him shaking. There's your father, Katie. A thirty-two-year-old West Texas hockey goon, who sent postcards to you when you were little, who once brought you presents at Christmas. Who now only sends checks to your mother. He sent her a thirteenth birthday card. He didn't call. He isn't really on Facebook anymore. Once, he learned, she posted something on the El Paso Storm team page, "That's my father," beneath a photo of him jamming two benders against the glass.

"Will you sing, Tim?" Father Larry says. Larry's looking at him. Larry's been done with the Bible for a while and they're all looking at him now. "I thought maybe you could sing something," Larry says again, like they know each other, like Oak's there all the time, like he's not like he is. His ma would sing a song when she was happy. Rod Stewart, Neil Diamond. She'd play *Dusty in Memphis* over and over, said Dusty Springfield was the best Irish singer outside of Donegal. She'd never been to Donegal. She'd swim without getting her cigarette wet, he remembers that, a group of them, waist-deep smoking in the water off L Street, flicking their butts at the waves. One time a life guard, Oak was maybe nine, the lifeguard seventeen, whistled at them and came down to the water's edge and told them they couldn't smoke in the water and they went to town on the kid whose balls must have risen up into his throat, his ma even going so far as to grab the kid and hump him from behind. They fell out laughing. The kid ran back up into his chair. His ma passed out the Marlboros and the women lit up dramatically and then she gave Oak a cigarette and he lit up too. Every mother on the beach was laughing. Send the lifeguard back to Quincy.

"No, Tim," Arlene says, dropping his hand.

"Let him sing," Auntie Ciara, the good one, his ma's sister who lives in Syracuse, New York, says.

"I will," Oak says.

He sang solos with Larry in the Our Lady choir. He still knows the old songs. His ma wasn't religious. She went to mass because she went to mass. If she nicked from the plate, she put back twice. She might do a line in the kitchen. She might go out with the girls from the hospital where she cut hair after Oak's father took his bottles and split.

Oak plants his feet in the muddy grass and sings—

> *Be Thou my Vision, O Lord of*
> *my heart;*
> *Naught be all else to me, save*
> *that Thou art.*

FOR THE MOMENT, JUST THAT, looking down into the hole, with his daughter somewhere behind him, with Jim Sharkey tall in the gray rain, his ma in a box, the birds up in the wet, leafless Boston trees. And then—in case his ma is watching, floating up above the town, having a smoke in the clouds, and for Kate's rebel blue hair—he looks over at his daughter and lets it fly.

> *Who's that knocking on my door? It's*
> *gotta be a quarter to four—*
> *Hot legs, you're wearing me out!*
> *Hot legs, you can scream and shout!*
> *Hot legs, are you still in school?*
> *I love you honey!*

3

Oak heads down Broadway, people eye-popping him, getting out of his way, he's big, his face is scarred and freshly scabbed, and his nose long ago became a flat mess. Past what was The Quiet Man, where his father and Shark took him for steak tips when he was a kid. Past an eight-story condo that blocks the church that was the last stop on the Holy Seven church walk. Past a new Starbucks, a new CVS, a new TD Bank. Yuppie bars—The Red Door, The Open Book, Boston Monty's—half the town has been taken over by money and Oak sure as shit could not blame them. Let them come: the lawyers and their doctor wives, the real estate tycoons.

Donahue's is still there, up above the embankment for the T-yard, and it's open at 10:00 a.m. Someone's thrown crumbs for the pigeons that flap around in front of a spray-painted memorial on Donahue's brick alley wall: RIP Mikey above a green Celtic cross and a flaming orange syringe.

Oak pushes through the barroom door. "Bud," he says and he drinks the beer in two swallows. "And Jack." And that goes down and the barman refills it in a way that Oak doesn't like, and he stares at the skinny bastard, forty or so, with a bluebird tattoo on his neck, the guy's skin already brown from smoking. Oak feels the Jack in the back of his heart, like his heart is on a hot pan, and the waves rush down his arms and into his hands that fist around the bar edge.

He couldn't stay, with Kate and Slats and Shannon, with Shark, with his sister holding his hand in the rain, with Kate crying into a tree. A procedure, his mother said over the phone in the summer. Something before you get breast cancer. *Not much material to work with*, she said. And, *If they kill me, I'll sue.*

Oak takes his shades off. He wipes his face with his sleeve. His suit is soaked, outside from the rain, inside from his sweat. He glances into the bar back mirror. The space around his right eye is black and purple and his face is red and scabbed around his beard. The Albuquerque guys did him pretty good. He deserved it. Oak looks into his own eyes. They float there, looking back, eyes into eyes and he sees Pat McDonald lying in a hospital bed in New Mexico, that eye shoved back in place, bright red. He looks away from his own reflection. Reflected beside him in the mirror is another bearded guy sitting at the bar who looks at him until their eyes meet, and an old man who's staring into the bar wood.

And a woman sat at the end of the bar, alone. The woman is dressed in a black suit, professional-looking, Asian, a little older than him. She sits in the shadow of the bar corner beneath a glowing beer clock. At ten in the morning. Oak sees that she's drinking coffee, at Donahue's, where her suit ought to be wrapped in plastic to protect it. Maybe, he thinks, Donahue is selling the place, if there even is a Donahue, and she's a prospective buyer. The woman is sort of staring into nothing, though, like the old man, and when she brings her coffee to her lips Oak sees that her hands are shaking.

He knows that shake. It could be booze. But it could be

something else. He'll shake himself awake at night, the next fight there in his head. He shakes in the morning from inside his bones. The woman looks up. Their eyes meet in the bar mirror. Her eyes are dark, like a swirl of wood. He realizes he's staring at her reflection. He nods at her in the mirror, feeling himself redden, he can see what she must be staring at in her eyes. She nods back as Oak looks away.

"Both again," Oak says to the barman. He gets his sunglasses back on.

When Kate was born he was skating in Providence. He took the bus home. They let him hold her. She was tiny in his arms and he was worried that he'd drop her, but she fit there. She smelled good—as a baby, as a little kid, today in his arms by the grave. He remembers that smell sometimes, at night, with his head ringing. He remembers the warm feeling. And then in the summer after his first year in Michigan when Kate was four, Slats and Shannon told him about Slats and Shannon and everyone decided it was best that he be like an uncle—Shannon's words—Kate's father yes but like an uncle, and so Oak sent money and visited at Christmases and summers before he stopped visiting entirely and the decade disappeared.

"You're Tim O'Connor."

Oak doesn't know if he's heard it outside or inside his head so he doesn't say anything, just stares ahead into the bar back mirror where the Asian woman looks up again with her dark eyes that are at once beautiful, even in the mirror, and far away.

"I used to see you play." It's the bearded guy. "I heard you were in Michigan."

"Visiting."

"Right, right. Me too. I'm up in Nashua now. My brother still lives on Gold Street, can you believe it?"

Oak doesn't want to talk.

"You could bang," the guy says, grinning.

She's staring at him in the mirror. He's watching her behind his shades.

"Ah shit, your mother died, right? My brother heard."

"Yeah."

"I'm sorry."

"Don't sweat it."

"She looked in on our grandmother."

And the old man is looking up now, too, and the bartender is coming over and a fat guy with a medical cane comes in the door, the sun out now and slashing in. Oak takes a quick breath. His whole face tightens. He blows it out.

"It's a shame, Oak."

Oak steps backward, stumbles a little, the lights of a shitty jukebox surprising some part of his head. He gets into the men's room. He gets water onto his face. Drinks some from his shaking hands. He leans on the sink, trying to breathe. He tries to breathe at night. He tries to breathe in ice baths. He tries to breathe on the bench.

The toilet stall door opens. A skinny guy fall-steps forward, popping against the bathroom wall. The guy starts steadily banging his forehead against the wall tile. There's a blood drop on his neck from where Oak figures he put the needle in.

Oak takes the guy's stick arm and eases him from the wall. The guy worms around. Oak leads him out of the bathroom and sits him at a table where the guy collapses, the jukebox lights swarming, the bass line hurting some place deep inside Oak's head. Oak hurries past the bar, past the Asian woman in her suit, and the bearded hockey fan, past the old man and the bartender, out into a bright slam of Boston sunlight.

He finds his phone. His fingers shake thickly across the glass. He sends a text to Major.

> How's McDonald?

He waits. It's 8:00 a.m. in Texas. Major texts back.

> Okay.

> Will he skate?

> Don't know. They dinged you for
> twenty-five games.

Oak looks across to the T-yard where his father worked with Shark under the trains and then later in an office. The train cars are silver and damp, the glassy downtown towers across the channel behind them like another world.

The phone buzzes in his hand. He looks down at it. The text from Major reads:

> You okay?

Oak's phone buzzes again. He squints at it.

> You there?

> Yeah. Thanks.

Can you talk?

                                                    No.

You got a call at team office. A guy
named Rob Kellet from Providence
College. You know him?

It's strange for Oak to see the name, Rob Kellet, to hear it inside of his head. Oak hasn't talked to Rob Kellet, their PC Friar defensive coach, since Providence. Ten years ago. The last time Oak saw Rob Kellet, they were sailing a stolen rowboat down the Providence River, pirate-waving a burning Brown University jersey as a flag, shooting empty beer cans from a stolen T-shirt gun to the people watching from the shore.

4

The Broadway Diner is unchanged, at the intersection of Broadway and Dorchester Avenue, the heart of the neighborhood, except for the Blue Bikes rack out front. He and Shannon did homework in the diner on weekends. There's a Police Athletic League sticker on the window, a Thanksgiving Turkey Drive poster, a placard for a Christmas Pageant at the Greek Orthodox Church.

Slats is waiting for him at the counter in his funeral suit and a green Kangol hat.

Oak sits. A picture of Red Auerbach still hangs over the cash register beside a signed photo of John Paul Cuniff in his BC uniform, framed.

"Here." Slats hands him a pint beneath the diner counter.

Oak takes a drink. He sets the bottle on the counter.

"You all right?" Slats grabs the pint and hides it away.

"Thanks for coming to the service," Oak says.

"I mean, with the way you took off," Slats says.

"I couldn't stand there anymore." Oak runs a hand along the counter, doesn't look at the guy who is raising his daughter.

"You look . . . like maybe things have been tough, huh?"

Oak shakes his head. "I'm good. I blew out my back last spring. Had a surgery. I'm good now." Slats hands him the bottle back. Oak shakes it off.

"She was a great one," Slats says.

"What's the job, Kevin?"

At the service Slats said he had a quick job for him. Oak knows that a quick job doesn't mean a good job or even a fully legal one, not with Slats. But he needs money. Money to eat, money to workout, money to skate. For pills. He doesn't have any savings. The suspension means his four hundred a week is gone.

"Straight to business, huh, Oak?" Slats's eyes narrow. "Because I haven't heard from you in a while, you know? A long while. None of us have. Kate for instance. No emails. No calls."

Oak can't do it now, have any kind of talk. It's only the beer and whiskey that is keeping him from puking out his body's need for painkillers. "What's the job, Kevin?" He says it fast. He looks to the waitress who brings him a tea. Oak lifts the cup with both hands, his hands are a mess, and lets the hot liquid burn some feeling back into his lips and tongue.

"I'm working a demolition site," Slats says, steadily.

He can do it. It's going to hurt, but he can do it. He'll make it back for the Texas League playoffs, if the team gets its shit together and wins some games. And then, thinking of this, the texts from Major about Rob Kellet come back into Oak's head. Oak gets his shades off, looks at his phone to make sure it happened. The texts are there.

Slats leans forward. "The place is loaded with copper, Oak. Copper wire. Copper pipes. We're stripping it. Throwing it into trucks. I said to Only, that's the guy I know, that I know a guy, big guy. Four hundred for three days, if we do it right. Rob Zink's working security."

Oak and Slats and sometimes Zinky did little jobs behind Oak's father's back for Uncle Barry as kids. Bring the Long Fellow these car keys. Run this envelope over to Fat Mitch.

"It's all insurance, Oak. The Georgians bought the building. The demo guys think they're getting the copper but we take it first. It's not on any books, no one's going to notice. Except the demo guys."

Oak crushes what's left in the tea bag with his spoon. Oak wonders what Rob Kellet wants. The last Oak heard, Kellet was coaching in Maine. "I got something going, Slats. I don't want to do something dumb."

"You saying I'm dumb now, Oak?"

"What kind of name is Only?"

"He's Georgian. You know, the country."

"My kneecaps are already busted."

Slats looks at him and Oak sees the years on his friend's face. He also sees in Slats something he can't name, something genuine and settled.

Oak stands. When he does his left hip goes soft and he lurches into the counter.

"Jesus, Oak—"

A couple cops look over.

"Get a genuine fucking job, will you? Will you do me that favor, Slats?"

Slats looks down into his coffee. "I got a real job. This is extra." Slats looks back up at Oak, and Oak sees his friend's face again, the face he ran with, skated with, cried with by the water when Slats's father died. He sees Slats taking Kate's hand at the funeral, sees again what is settled in his eyes.

"I need the money," Slats says. But there's something else in there, Oak thinks, the same Slats bullshit that always came around. "You don't got kids, Oak. I mean . . . you fucking know what I mean. It costs money. Shannon's working half-time at a doctor's office. Shannon needs to be home, Oak. With how Kate can be."

"Why'd you bring Kate, Slats?"

"Here we go."

"I just want to know—"

"Margaret was her grandmother, Oak. Kate wanted to go."

"You kept her from my mother."

"Oak. Your mother didn't want to see her, all right? We tried."

"Bullshit."

"Talk to your sister about your mother."

"I want to see her." Oak says it fast.

Slats slows, his voice is steady and quiet again. "No one's stopping you, Tim."

Oak turns to look at the street. "I gotta get cleaned up. I gotta get a car." He looks back.

Slats is looking at him now like there's something there to pity. "Just show up, Tim," Slats says. Oak isn't sure what he means. Then Slats says, "St. Joe's in Savin Hill. I'll text you the time. I need the money, Oak. We do. It's all insurance."

"St. Joe's? We used to play them." Oak shakes his head.

Slats smiles a little. "Churches and catholic schools are hot. I'm not saying it's right, Oak. But they are."

5

Oak leans against a signpost outside the diner, gets his left ankle into his left hand, bends his foot up behind him to his ass. He takes a fast breath. He snaps his kneecap back into place. He squats, gets his hip bone aligned in its socket.

His grandfather lived in Savin Hill, his grandfather who Oak knows beat the shit out of his father. His father took Oak to Shark's gym. His father could fight. And his father could skate. Oak's father figure-skated all through high school—they had a photo on the mantel over their bricked-up fireplace, Oak's father spinning in the air—and he boxed which probably kept the bullies away. And his parents could ballroom dance and that's what had made his father so good in the ring. Oak's parents won all kinds of dancing awards. It's how they met. They competed in club leagues around New England and New York. Oak loved to see his parents dancing: his old man wide and big, but quicker on his feet than guys twenty pounds lighter; his ma small and energetic, the two of them sweeping around in each other's arms, grinning at each other, him and Arlene cheering them on from a table where they had ginger ales and Cokes.

Oak walks up Telegraph to the park. At the base of the hill-
top monument, Boston spreads around him: the harbor and the
JFK library, the Tobin Bridge, the Prudential and John Hancock
skyscrapers across the channel. Oak walks around the base of the
monument to the Battle of Southie where the colonists beat back
the British, the monument spindling the gray November sky.
"One big prick on a hill," his father called the monument. "We're
waving our dickie at the Crown."

Oak drinks from the pint Slats gave him. When he saw Kate
four years back it was a train wreck, with her saying nothing, Shannon gently crying, and Slats—fucking Slats—looking like he'd
pissed himself in the confessional. That was around the time when
Oak first realized he was starting to forget things. His ATM pin.
The names of old teammates. Slats and Shannon drove Kate down
from Lynn to his ma's for Christmas. He was skating in Florida
then and he brought her a four-foot stuffed alligator that took up
the whole overhead compartment on the plane. He can't remember
what she talked about, when they did talk. He's tried, but he can't.
He remembers they didn't stay long at his ma's. He remembers Slats
taking Kate out of their house by the hand. Oak kissed his daughter good-bye, and she looked at him as she walked away with Slats,
over her shoulder, Shannon lingering to kiss Oak on the cheek, his
ma standing next to him as he watched them take off, Oak going
upstairs to soak his dumb body in an ice bath. He watched her
from the bathroom window like a coward. Fade out, fade in. Come
to on the team bench, on the bus, in this park on a hill.

There's a bum on one of the park benches. There's a girl jog-
ging while talking on her phone. The bum's talking in his sleep,
drifting his arms over his head. He's got a beard that runs all over
his face and neck with food in it and a bottle in a bag.

Oak finishes the Jack standing. He resists the urge to heave the bottle at the bum. Oak lies on the park grass and lets the sky spin. There's a cop now over by the bum on the bench. The cop's a chest-out kid, peach fuzz, giving the bum the kind of look that says, This is your lucky day, *son*, I'm going to give you a chance to move on. Like the bum's doing anything. Like the bum isn't just sleeping.

Join the T, the Coast Guard, the electrician's union. Get an MBA. Insurance. Real Estate. Construction. Massport and the TSA. Everyone knew someone. They remember him. They remember him for youth hockey, for Silver Gloves, skating for St. Ant's in West Roxbury, for PC, pounding the shit out of the BU team that eventually won the Beanpot, Oak touching the puck on all three goals, scoring the second. His mother put the headlines up over the mantel. The photos from *The Herald* and *The Globe*. He didn't run. His father ran. Oak had a chance to do the one thing he could do well, the one thing that made sense to him, that was fun. He's loved skating for as long as he can remember. He loved street hockey on rollerblades, crash a kid over the snow banks, smack him into the Farragut park boards. Slap the puck into the net. Go out after for soda and burgers, with the kids you just knocked on their asses. He carried a stick when he was little all around the house. His father set up a net in the driveway. They let him organize the rental skates at Murphy Rink, sweep up a little, in exchange for free ice, when they saw how he could rip.

When the bum doesn't move and, Oak thinks, why the fuck should he?, the punk cop pokes at the bum with his club. The bum's whole face shakes. The bum could be any age. The cop pokes the bum harder, enough to freak the guy out.

"Yo. Leave him the fuck alone—"

It just comes out. Oak tries to stand but all at once he can't. The cop's coming over, shaking his head.

Oak feels his fists ball. He's sitting now on the grass.

"You his friend?" the cop says.

They sent him out against the rookies sometimes, the pretty boys on their way up to Carolina or Grand Rapids. To test them. Oak is the tester. At first he liked it okay and then quickly he didn't. Word about him got around the high school parking lots. In West Roxbury. In Medford. Good Catholic boys. They put him on websites, they put him on Jumbotrons. In Texas, in Florida, in Carolina, in Michigan, guys would come up and ask him to fight: at bars, in parking lots, at parties. They *wanted* him to bust their faces so they could take a picture and Instagram their friends. He could still skate as well as them, better. Soul-skate, not technical. He's looking up at the cop. His heart is pounding now, the muscles behind his eyes tightening. The sun and his brain make the cop flicker.

"You got ID?" the cop asks.

"No."

"Will you get out of here?"

"I was born here."

The Catholic league trophies, Arnie's Army, *fuck Cushing Academy*, the pictures in the papers, the pass to PC: Grand Rapids on a contract with the Red Wings' AHL team, Wilmington for the ECHL. Tampa and Jacksonville. Kate was three when he went to Michigan, four when Slats came on the scene, nine when Oak slid down the east coast. Ten years gone. The punch-ups and the money not coming. The drinking to sleep slowing him down. The fights beating him up, the drinking to keep fighting, then the pills—up and down—the brain-aches, the blackouts, and the long fall to El Paso.

Behind the cop, the bum's still freaking out over the jab to the ribs, grabbing and brushing at his side like something's gnawing at his flesh. Oak stands. His legs hold.

He's decked the kid before he knows he's done it.

The cop collapses. The cop's got his gun out and Oak knows he is fucked, fucked, fucked, and then Oak's howling, and he's spitting mucus and he can't breathe and he can't see out of his already fucked eyes.

TWO COPS DRIVE HIM IN A SQUAD CAR toward the power station not far from his house. Another cop came and took the cop he dropped away. The cop that's driving pulls the car over. There's no one around. Oak's hands are cuffed behind his back.

The cops get out of the car. Oak knows what's coming. They get in the back seat and do him fast, a white cop punching him straight in the face, the black cop hesitating until Oak delivers a headbutt to his nose.

6

Flying at the net, the goalie's going to splay, dude thinks Oak's going five-hole, but he's going top right, deke, deke, forehand, backhand, forehand, the goalie goes down and Oak sees it in the goalie's body, the goalie tries to stand even as he slides, realizing too late his mistake, as Oak snipes the corner, a black streak past the goalie's falling face, the red light cherrying the air. Oak's flying and he's waking and the goal light is a smoke detector hanging off a concrete ceiling, stuck there by tape.

Oak's alone, uncuffed, in a small room at the station house. He was in emergency overnight, and then he saw a judge, and now he's here. He needs to get his shirt off. The thing is still drenched with pepper, like his face is inches from peppers frying in oil. He needs a drink and he needs to piss. They did him big-time in the squad car. Too big. He doesn't blame them. He's not going to finger them. Oak remembers an ambulance taking the cop he decked away. He remembers being hand-cuffed and hauled into a squad car, then driven down behind the power station where two other cops added onto what was already there. Then the emergency room. Time in a hospital bed. Then a judge. There's blood with the sweat in his eye. He remembers Kate at the funeral, singing "Hot Legs" for her blue hair and for his ma, and now he remembers Slats and the diner and the walk up the hill. He remembers Rob Kellet. It's the next day.

The doors open. "Oak—" And there's a face he sort of knows. Neat, tall, and bald.

"I'm sorry about your mother, Tim."

The guy means it and Oak recognizes the cop, Peter MacIvoy, the Flying Scot that played in the adult leagues when Oak was a teen.

"Mac." He feels like a child. "I'm . . . sorry about all this."

"I know it, Tim."

The cops that beat him in the squad car step in behind Mac, looking like soft teenagers. Oak mashes his feet to the station house floor.

"How's your head?" Oak says to the white cop who Oak remembers from looking at him that he somehow got a boot into.

"Shut the fuck up," the punk says.

"You can't hit an officer, Oak," Mac says. "Though I'm guessing he deserved it."

Mac looks steadily at the two young cops. They look nervous. They should look nervous. They overdid it. In the police station bathroom he saw how fucked he is. Even though some of what they did was already done.

"So, you'll walk now and keep it clean, Oak. See the new lawyer."

"Sure, Mac."

His own voice sounds bad, his words slur together. He's got

nothing against cops. The cops in Grand Rapids and El Paso came to the games, came out afterward, bought him beers and tequila. As a kid, the Southie cops boxed with him at Shark's gym. That's how he knows Mac. But some of them, like the one in the park, are punks, and Oak knows that Mac knows this even as Mac has to protect his own.

Oak gets the crutches they gave him in emergency for his hip and Mac helps him out of the small room and down what feels like a long, glassy tube. The faces around him blur, the women at their desks, the kids in handcuffs. The Thanksgiving Food Drive table. A Boston Strong mural on the station house wall.

"Jim Sharkey's waiting for you," Mac says.

"Shark?"

"Outside." Mac puts a hand on Oak's shoulder and Oak jumps back.

"Hey, Tim—"

It's become a reflex, that flinch that keeps him in the game.

"I'll put in a good word. I remember what you did with the kids. And in the ring."

Oak nods. He used to skate around with the PAL peewees and midgets when he was in high school, tumble around, teach them trick shots, dumb shit. The coaches wanted to beat the kids into mini-pros but Oak figured the kids just wanted to have some fun.

"And be careful of that shit in your pocket."

Mac means the dozen Tramadol they gave him at the hospital to take home. Not refillable. He chewed four in the station house men's room. He's got enough Oxy left for maybe a week. He's going to need more. Oak backs out through the station house. It's raining again. He feels like he could be jumped. He sees Shark standing outside on the sidewalk. Shark stands tall in a raincoat, Shark's big glasses catching puddles and light, a black umbrella in his big black mitt. The Great Black Shark who coached him to the Silver Mittens when he was ten, Oak knocking a kid from Charlestown over the ropes when he was nine.

Oak gets down the wet station house steps. The crutches make walking a horror show.

"Jesus Christ, Tim."

"I'm all right."

Shark stares at him.

The doctor from yesterday said he might piss blood for a while and that his right knuckle was fucked. "There is prior damage," the doctor said. He's pissed blood before.

"I don't want this nonsense, Oak."

"I need a drink, Shark."

Shark reaches into his raincoat pocket, hands Oak a pint in a bag.

"You're in trouble, Tim."

Oak screws the cap off, takes a hit, sloshes his mouth to wake up, to get the burning done. Swallows. He needs to think straight.

"Assault and battery on police officers. *Local* police officers. Resisting arrest."

"They did me bad."

"You knocked one into Sunday."

Oak thinks to check his fists. He is able to make a fist with each hand. He can hold a stick. He drinks some more. He feels the sick rising in him.

"I don't understand you, Oak. Slipping away from your own mother's funeral. Singing songs."

He's not going to puke in front of Shark. But then he is, and he hustles to a gap beside the station house and heaves a belly-ful of nothing. He looks down to it, the alley wet with trash. He rests his head against the station house wall. The rain is like a shower that runs right through him so that he's cold even inside his blood. He shivers against it and the alley goes blank.

"Now's as good a time as any to tell you we're going down the street to a church." Shark is right next to him, sticking, that's how Shark taught him to box, stick to your opponent, don't let him slip away. "We're stopping in on a meeting," Shark says.

Oak finds a bourbon bottle in his hand, remembers puking, pours the rest of the bourbon down into his flapping gut. Holds it in there, pressing down with his will.

Oak hands the empty bottle back to Shark. "Thanks."

"They've helped some people, Tim. Helped me. Don't let this business fool you," Shark says, nodding at the empty bottle.

Oak lets Shark lead him across and down the street, past the pizza places, the laundromat. Sometimes Shark would run with him when Oak was a teenager. They'd run down along the water and up through the streets of Southie. Shark could really tear, and now they were side by side again, humping toward a small red-doored church with neat green bushes planted at its granite steps.

Shark holds open the church door. Incense rolls out across them. For a second, Oak stands on the church steps in the rain. He could give it all up, he thinks. Skating. The game. His life. He shivers it off. He feels the whole of the days, the bright-angled fear, the waking-up pain in his beat-down body, his slow-beating heart, the bitter taste of booze and puke and chewed-up Tramadol, the adrenaline drying inside him, turning his blood to acid.

Oak gets inside.

"We're going downstairs," Shark says, holding open a wooden basement door.

Oak leans the useless crutches against the wall. "A miracle," he manages to say to Shark. He limps toward the stairs.

His father gave it up once. Went to AA, said the meetings *compelled* him to take up drinking again. Oak remembers laughing at that as a kid. The Irish obligation. Oak had his first drink when he was eleven, out of Slats's mother's cabinet when Slats watered down her vodka and stole it for them. She knew it and blamed her boyfriend who backhanded Slats, but sort of laughed about it, too.

The basement meeting has already begun. A couple people turn when he and Shark enter the room. Oak sees the looks on their faces, trying not to be judgmental, staring quickly back into their laps or at the woman who's talking looking like a ghost.

There's no way he's sitting in that circle. He's grateful to Shark, for the concern, but he can't sit in that circle, he can't sit in it even if he wanted to, which he sure as fuck doesn't. He heads back up the basement stairs.

He gets inside the quiet of the church and sits in a pew.

LATER, OAK'S WATCHING RAIN DRIP DOWN the sorrowful mother with swords in her heart.

"You were snoring so loud I heard you from the stairs."

It takes him a minute. "What's up?" he says to Shark, who's standing over him.

"Do you know where you are?" Shark asks.

"I got hit."

"You didn't. Well, you did, but now you're in a church pew, Tim."

Brain working, pain working. He looks around. He's got to laugh. It hurts. But he's got to laugh.

"It's not funny, Tim."

"Bless me, Shark, for I have sinned."

"I tell you, you're in trouble, Oak."

"Tell me your sins, boyo."

Shark starts laughing too.

"The church'll straighten you out," Oak continues. "There's nothing our Lord and Savior can't do. Just look around at the joy of the world. Hey, Shark, you remember that time I knocked you flat out? I was, what, sixteen? I saw it so good: in slow motion. Just like you said. You checked something out in your office from the ring, a glance, but I saw it, your chin floating there like a fat black melon. Southpaw. Slo-mo. Pow!"

"You cracked my tooth. I had to get a goddamn crown."

"I was king! Crown!"

"You *was* king," Shark says, low. "And now?"

"King Oak. And you know it was the legs, the footwork. I hit you with footwork. Like you said. Legs, waist, shoulders, fist. That's how I hit McDonald. From the legs. It went right through, Shark. Came out the other side. That's what I tried to do. You know?" Oak hears himself say it. "Punch through his head."

"Come by the gym tomorrow, Tim. Come by sober. You got money?"

"But not like that."

Shark hands Oak two tens. "Go back to your mother's and go to bed. Don't think about it, Oak, do it. Come by tomorrow after you wake up. And eat something."

He hears Shark's hip pop as Shark walks away.

Oak sits in the silence, sits with the hum inside his head. He's on a bench, he's in the box. Five for roughing. Ten for fighting. He should have done it. Raised Kate. He could have done it. But he didn't.

7

Oak stands alone in the small waiting room outside the public defender's office, just up from the glassy Moakley Courthouse with a view for the defendants of the shining new harbor-front hotels. He's embarrassed that he doesn't have money to pay for a lawyer. But he's not going to ask Arlene for help.

He put on the suit he wore to the funeral, the suit he wore to cut a ribbon at a car lot in El Paso. When he called the legal aid office, the receptionist told him he'd been assigned a new lawyer, not the kid that was at his bail hearing. The new lawyer's name is Joan Linney.

"She's very good," the receptionist told him over the phone, like the receptionist was letting him in on a secret. "She works for a big firm in Back Bay." The receptionist went on to say how it was unusual to even meet with your public defender before trial, let alone one as "connected," but that Mrs. Linney wanted to meet with him personally.

He's standing in the waiting room, because his spine won't sit.

Joan Linney comes out of the office. She's carrying a mug

of coffee. She's Asian. Tall. She has silver barrettes in her thick black hair. She looks professional, smart—like the good-looking lawyer doing pro bono that she apparently is—except for the dark rings around her dark eyes.

"Mr. O'Connor?"

Oak sees her look him up and down. Studying him. Then, in a flash, he realizes that she is the woman from Donahue's bar who watched him with her hazy eyes in the bar mirror when he was there after his mother's funeral at ten o'clock in the morning.

"Come in," she says. He stands there. He's not sure what to say, or if to say anything. She does not seem to recognize him. He doesn't know if he would like him to say how he recognizes her, drinking off her shakes or buying the place or whatever she was doing.

She leads him into the office. There's another lawyer there, an older guy, Paul Newman in *The Verdict*, at a second desk. She introduces them. She motions for him to sit. Oak makes like it's not a problem to sit in the hard metal chair.

Joan looks at his file on her laptop. "Resisting arrest, obstruction, felony assault and battery on two police officers."

He realizes that she doesn't recognize him. He's thinking now maybe that it isn't even her, that his mind is playing a new kind of trick on him. He closes his eyes and opens them.

"If they want it, you're looking at five years."

She's staring at him but also beyond him to the far wall. It's unsettling. The other lawyer is pretending to look at his laptop but he can tell the guy is watching.

"But they don't seem to want it," she goes on. "Why?"

"Look at me."

He sees her eyes focus on his face.

He puts on a bit of the brogue for her. "They done me good, Mrs. Linney."

"This isn't a joke, Mr. O'Connor."

Oak stands. "This whole thing's a joke, Mrs. Linney. From the top of my busted head, to the bottom of my flat, black-toed feet. A fucking joke."

"Hey buddy." The other lawyer is eyeing him.

Oak's pacing, shaking his hands. Joan gets up from the desk. "How about a coffee, Mr. O'Connor?" she says.

He balls and unballs his fists. He suddenly can't even remember hitting the cop. Then he can. "I don't really drink it, believe it or not."

"I've got tea."

"I'm good."

She goes and gets him a mug of hot water, puts in a tea bag, comes to stand beside him.

"Special Korean tea. Good for the nerves." She hands him the mug.

He's not sure she's not fucking with him. But he drinks some, and the tea feels good down his throat. She's standing there beside him.

"Were you provoked?" she says.

"Yes."

She nods at him, like this was important for her to hear and to understand. He was provoked. He was sitting in the sun in the park he's been to since he was a boy.

Joan returns to the desk. He's still standing with the mug of tea.

"Are there witnesses?"

He thinks back to the bum. "No."

"What happened?"

"I just wanted to lay my head down."

"And?"

"That's it." He knows it sounds stupid.

"You didn't get up when the officer asked you to?" She makes a note in her laptop.

"These legs, they aren't just from the police."

"I know."

"Two guys couldn't do all this to me, Mrs. Linney."

She surprises him with a smile. Her teeth are fucked up so they have that, he thinks, and Donahue's, in common. "You played hockey, I understand. A bit of a local legend."

"I still play."

She nods. "The assistant DA, who's a schmuck, wants to cut you a break, maybe because of the hockey, maybe because he wants a quick win. Both probably."

She pulls a photo from a file folder. She hands it to him. Her fingernails are specked with some kind of paint. "They won't drop the assault and battery."

Oak looks at the photo. It's the cop he dropped. The cop's nose is bandaged, and his eyes are blackened. Oak shuts his own eyes against it. He wonders if she knows about Pat McDonald.

"A year if you accept a plea fast. A good chance at three if you don't."

"Some choice."

"It's easiest if we go with the year."

"We."

"I'm sorry."

"And I don't have any money."

"This is pro bono, Tim. My firm does this as a service, to give back."

"I didn't take anything of yours, Ms. Linney. So you don't need to give me anything back."

The other lawyer laughs at this.

"It's an obnoxious term," she says. "I'm sorry. I work with obnoxious people."

Oak laughs.

"I was raised in Newton, too, to make matters worse," she says about the rich Boston suburb.

Oak puts the photo of the cop back on her desk. He sits.

She looks at the laptop, then again at him. "The DA is generous right now. He wants to bury this. If I push him too much, if the case grows, goes on, then he has to save face. *The Herald* will pick it up."

"How long do I have to decide?"

"There's a hearing set for January."

"You paint or something?"

She looks at him.

"You got paint on your fingers."

Joan shrinks back.

"I'm sorry," Oak says. "I didn't mean to talk about anything."

"It's fine."

"I'm saying stupid shit. Doing stupid shit. I know it. But it's going away. I'm getting back to where I want to be. The funeral, my mother. It's a setback." He's looking at his hands.

She seems to be thinking. She speaks carefully, like what she is about to say is also important to her. "I'm painting my house."

"How's it going?"

"Not good."

She reaches into a BC Eagles gym bag. She lifts a camera from the bag. She comes around the desk.

"Would it be okay if I take some photos?"

"Okay."

She snaps one, checks the camera's view finder. She stares into it for too long.

"That bad?" he says, trying to make a joke because it feels weird, having his picture taken by someone he doesn't know, someone who is going to use the photos in court to show how fucked up he is.

"No." She takes another. "Excuse me." She checks it. Then, quickly, she says, "I need you to, I'm sorry to ask this, take off your shirt."

"I hardly know you, Mrs. Linney." And knowing, immediately, that somehow this was the wrong thing to say.

She steps backward, turns toward her desk. "You're right. I'm sorry. Al can take them. I wouldn't have asked if he wasn't here."

The other lawyer nods. "Yeah, I can do it."

"We're good," Oak says.

He lifts his jacket off. He feels every inch of his right shoulder. He digs his feet into the carpet, jams his teeth into his gums. He's not going to show her, he's not going to show anyone how he feels, what it takes to remove his jacket, how for a couple years now he has had a hard time getting his fingers to work his shirt buttons. He turns from her. He undoes his shirt. He hears both lawyers tapping keys. In a mirror on the opposite side of the room he sees Joan reflected again, watching him. He can't get the last button undone on his shirt. He pulls the shirt apart and the button pops to the rug. He hangs the shirt with his jacket on the metal chair.

He lifts his T-shirt, feeling the dull aching misconnect between his lumbar spine and the atlas at the base of his brain. He squeezes his legs to stand there. "Oh," he hears Joan say behind him, the sound jumping from her. He peels the T-shirt over his head, his shoulder jawing, drops it on the chair and turns back to face them. He can see how he looks in their faces. She is standing in front of her desk.

"I'm sorry, Tim," she says, and she touches his scarred shoulder with the tips of fingers. He looks at them there, her slender fingers on his skin. He looks at her. Her eyes are glossy from lack of sleep but her face feels open and warm. Then quickly she pulls her hand away.

"You didn't do it," he says.

Joan flashes six pictures. Then two more. "Got it," she says. He wonders what it is.

She zips her camera back into her BC bag. He doesn't bother with his T-shirt. He gets his dress shirt back on. She's watching him struggle.

"Go Eagles," he says, to say something.

"My husband," Joan says. "A BC homer through and through."

He feels his sweat sticking to the shirt. The office feels smaller. The other lawyer is shaking his head in a way Oak doesn't like.

"I want you to bring me whatever photos you can find of you skating as a kid. Newspaper clippings, that kind of thing. Stuff that makes you look good."

"You don't have to do this."

"I've asked for video from the park. And from the squad car. I don't know if I'll get them. I'll call you when I know more. And I don't have an address listed for you," Joan says, looking at her notes.

"I'm staying at my mother's."

"What's the address?"

He can't remember. "I don't know."

She stiffens a little when he says this.

"You think a guy who punches out a cop is a nice guy, Mrs. Linney?"

"No," she says. "I don't."

"Margaret O'Connor on East Third Street," Oak says when it comes back to him. "Eleven East Third Street. There's a landline. If she answers call the church because you've got a miracle on your hands." He grabs his coat from the chair and goes.

8

Oak waits on the pharmacist at CVS. He doesn't have any script, but he's got the team doctor's office number on his phone. The team's doctor doesn't care if he comes in face-to-face. The doctor won't give him Oxy anymore, but he gives him Tramadol and Vicodin in Texas-sized portions which Oak and the doctor know he needs. There's a pregnant mother in line with him and an old couple. The mother's on her phone.

"They don't have a prescription for you on file, Mr. O'Connor," the pharmacist says. "You'll have to call them yourself."

St joe's in savin hill isn't much, three brick stories with a small parking lot out front and what was a playground, now empty, to the side. Not much of a church, not much of a school, it's in the big shadow of BC High down the road. Whenever they played them in middle school, Coach Langley played the bench—a Catholic charity. Savin Hill, where Oak's father's father lived when Oak was little, his grandfather sitting on his porch in his skully, talking about fishing in Yarmouth and Athlone, shaking his head at the newcomers, meaning the blacks and the PRs. Savin Hill. Stab 'n Kill. Oak's grandmother moved on to Bourne where Oak guesses she's smoking herself to death in a lawn chair by the Cape Cod Canal.

There's a temporary chain link fence around the school ahead of the demolition. Oak finds Slats on the front steps talking with Tom Zink. Oak knows Zink well enough to say hello, not well enough for more than that. Zink's wearing a security jacket and a hat with earflaps against the cold.

Oak follows Slats down the school stairs into a basement furnace room, a network of copper pipes along the school ceiling. There's two white guys, Russians or Georgians, and two Mexican guys. No one's talking English. Everyone's smoking. The fat, tanned Russian, what's left of his hair oiled, maybe in his forties, looks him over, frowns, looks at Slats.

"You say he's okay?" the fat Russian says to Slats. Oak figures this is Only.

"He's more than okay."

"He looks like shit."

"He's standing right here," Oak says.

The guy grins. "That's clever. And true. I'm Only."

"Oak."

"Ivan, introduce yourself."

A big wideo in a track suit with a nose that's been flattened from fists nods at Oak. "I am Ivan."

Oak puts his hand out and the guy shakes it.

"He's the hockey player, yes?" Ivan asks.

"Yes," Only says.

No one introduces the two Mexican guys, so Oak introduces

himself, using some of the Spanish he's picked up in Texas and Florida.

"I will be by tomorrow," Only says. "Do what Ivan says. We finish in three days." Only and Slats head toward the stairs. Something doesn't feel right. Oak follows after them. Oak puts a hand down hard on Only's shoulder. He sees Slats eyes widen slightly when he does it.

"What is all this?" Oak says to both of them.

"Oak—" Slats says.

Oak squeezes Only's big shoulder. His knuckles feel like they might tear though the skin, but he wants the message to be received. "I can't get busted."

Only looks at him, steadily. Oak sees he's older than he thought, maybe closer to sixty. His teeth are yellow, and he's got some kind of oil on his face, like he's trying to stay young or else is sweating out Russian Crisco. He's tan, in November.

"Your friend said you are reliable and could use some lolly. He also mentioned your hockey stardom. I love the game and always wished I was big like you so I could well play it. If you do not want this job, Oak, please, go now. It is not a problem."

Only looks at Oak for a little longer, nods, then walks away up the basement stairs.

Slats waits until the guy is gone. "I need this job, Oak. I'm not getting any work. Shannon wants Kate to do hip-hop dancing classes for fuck's sake."

"I can pay for that," he says quickly.

Slats looks at him.

"Okay," Ivan says behind them. "Let's make it happen."

Oak goes back into the furnace room and picks up his hammer, crowbar, and wrench.

THERE ARE CAMERAS EVERYWHERE, so Only must want to have video of them in action. Oak's got to control his body. He's got to shut it up. He's got to work out and get skating. He's got to make some money to eat and pay his uncle Barry for what he needs.

"You know how to do this?" The big Mexican with the mustache, Esteban, asks.

"No."

"Here." Esteban gets up on one of the step ladders. He wrenches a pipe joint. "Twist and pull." The pipe slides from the joint. Esteban comes down the ladder, moves it to the next joint. He gets himself back up the ladder, wrenches the joint, grabs the copper pipe, and throws it to the tarp he's got spread on the basement floor. "It's not the Mona Lisa," Esteban says, and Oak's not sure if he means what they're stealing or what they're doing. Oak gets a ladder and the wrench. The ladder wavers. He climbs it like a little kid. When he grips a pipe joint, his shoulder feels knifed. He's not getting through it without what's left in his pocket and he's not going to get through the week without Uncle Barry. Oak grabs the two 40s, chews them, tastes the sweet powder go bitter on his tongue.

SLATS IS RIGHT. No one cares that they are there. They hurl the copper onto tarps, haul the tarps out to a box truck that's parked inside the temporary fence. Zink leans on the front of the building, playing on his phone. Ivan, who explained how he is Russian and how Only is a Georgian asshole, spends the morning smoking in the cab of his pickup truck.

Esteban is from Monterrey. He's big and fat and has three kids in Mexico. Going where the work is, Oak figures. When the basement pipes are down and loaded, Esteban brings out a bag lunch and a thermos of coffee. They sit on the box truck's rear bumper, away from the bay wind in the sun. Esteban pours Oak some coffee into a plastic cup that he's got with him in his lunch bag, like the guy prepared to share his meal. Esteban's lunch is some kind of meat wrapped in corn tortillas. The coffee's got booze in it.

"Not bad," Oak says to him.

Esteban smiles. He speaks his English slowly. "When you live without a woman, you live with a bottle."

"That's poetry," Oak says.

Esteban smiles wider.

"When I worked in the car factory, we write poetry and read it to whoever wanted to listen. Which was not too many people!"

Esteban tears one of his tortilla sandwiches in half, hands it to Oak.

Oak takes it. It's pork mole. "Mole," Oak says.

Esteban nods.

Oak tells him about the mole at Rosa's in El Paso before Rosa's son was found stabbed dead in a dumpster. Esteban nods again. Pours them more spiked coffee. "My Melinda, her sister?—" Esteban makes a motion with his hand, Oak figuring she's dead. "And her brother? He's not dead yet, but he will be. They cook it up in a plastic jug. Boom."

Oak doesn't know if Esteban means the jug or their heads but either way he's right.

"I work here until December, then go home for two months, come back when construction begins again. My little one, Jan, she wants a confirmation dress. And Cristi, *quinceañera* . . ."

Esteban's in jeans and a Nike sweater and a wool hat. Oak pictures Esteban every morning on the bus from Eastie, then an hour on the T, sleeping on a sofa if he's lucky, making his sandwiches, drinking his bad tequila. One day to the next. So his kid can go to a school where she won't get shot. So he can see his wife.

Esteban balls the cellophane the tortillas were wrapped in, tosses the cellophane to the dirt.

"Here," Esteban says. "Jan."

Esteban's wallet is stuffed two-inches thick, wrapped with a rubber band. She's eight. Smiling.

She's sitting on a low stone wall.

Her black bangs hang in her bright eyes.

Oak thinks of the picture that's on his mother's mantel, of Kate when she was little, Shannon pulling her blue sled through the snow.

"She's very beautiful," Oak says.

"Yes," Esteban says, smiling, nodding, carefully slipping the photo back into his wallet.

Ivan gets out of his running truck. Smoking, he takes a leak, his piss steaming up the cold air. They go back inside to join Slats and the other Mexican pulling copper wires from the school's old walls.

9

Oak wakes in his boyhood bed, headboardless, footboardless, the sunlight kicking his head. Oak thinks he has to get up to practice then remembers where he is. He drops to the floor and lies there, as he does every morning, waiting for his spine and his hip and his shoulder to reset. Lying there, he sees Joan Linney's face behind her camera, looking at him. She looks scared. He sees her sitting alone in Donahue's bar. He gets up and goes into the bathroom. His mother's blood is still in the tiles from where she fell. He covers the dried blood with Ajax. He gets to his knees and scrubs his mother's blood away with a washcloth. Oak stands. Steadies his legs again. She's there on the washcloth, what's left of her blood. He sees McDonald's blood on the ice and his own blood down his face, in Albuquerque, in the squad car, in everywhere. When he was ten he took an uppercut at the gym that ran his top tooth through his lower lip. Shark bandaged it. Oak liked the look, it made him look good. When he came home, his ma gave him a half-shot of Powers and had one herself. Oak turns the sink tap on. He washes the thin trace of her blood down the pipes and out into South Boston Bay. He goes downstairs for a shake of whey protein, Jack, and eggs.

IN THE AFTERNOON, IT SNOWS. A light November snow. Oak's at the kitchen table making a list of what he needs to do. The snow's beautiful. He missed it in Texas, in Florida, in Carolina. He'd sled in the small park up the road as a kid. Stuck his tongue on a lamp-post. Sled-raced his father down to the power plant where the cops did him in. As a kid, all he wanted to do was skate. Street hockey in the summer, ice hockey in the winter, rinks all year round. Oak turned his room into a rink. He'd talc the floor and sock skate, knocking his pals over the furniture.

That night, he drags the old hockey net up from the crawl space under the house and sets it up in the driveway. He finds an old stick and a basketful of pucks. He dumps the basket of pucks in the driveway. Real pucks, street pucks, roller pucks, all beat to shit. He can't find the plastic launch pad he had but he sets the first puck on an ice patch for effect.

Oak brings the stick back to his waist, his shoulder holding, and roofs the puck. Another. The next. He takes a drink. Sets up three more pucks. Corner, corner, five-hole, the stick-slap bouncing off the cold cement, the cold house walls, the cold, quiet street. A light comes on in the house next door. He sees a shadow up in the window. The house is being renovated. There's a sign in front and an Acura in the driveway. The Welshes are long gone. Oak sets three more pucks onto the patch of ice. Lasers one into the upper left corner of the net. Upper right. He brings the last puck, a street-roller, back to where the driveway meets the road. Forehand, backhand, he dekes up the slanted driveway, spins, and stuffs it past the imaginary tender.

BREATHING HARDER THAN HE SHOULD, Oak drinks some beer. He finds Rob Kellet's phone number on his phone and sits on the front steps. He calls Kellet. It's midnight.

After a short catch up—Kellet was at U Maine after PC and has now stepped up to D-coach for the ECHL Worcester Rockets—Kellet gets down to it.

"We're lacking spine, Oak."

"Tom Bowie, my coach in Texas, thinks you heard about my fight in Albuquerque."

There's silence on the other end. "I'm not going to lie, Oak. The team did. Word travels. It's online."

"It's fucked up."

"I know what you can do, Oak. Who you are. This is an opportunity, Oak."

"I wish that never happened."

"No doubt. How long are you home for?"

"Home?"

"In Boston."

"I'm suspended until January."

"Can you come up early December?"

"Tell them I can skate, Robbie."

"We all know what you can do, Tim."

10

Oak takes the T for a half hour to a rink in Quincy so no one he knows can see him suck. He's not going to skate at Murphy's Rink in Southie, where he skated as a kid, where his picture still hangs on the wall of fame.

The girl at the Quincy skate counter is maybe sixteen. Oak leans on the counter to hold himself up.

"What size?" the girl asks.

"Fourteen."

"We don't have a lot. Try these."

She brings him a pair of thickly padded Reebok, cheap shit for a fat guy.

"Those are too soft."

"You should *try* them." She smiles.

He points at a decent-looking pair of Bauers that he's not sure why they've got. "Give me those."

"They're twelves."

"I'll suck in my breath."

She smiles again.

He pays her. He goes over to the benches.

His father took him to midnight skates. His father used the trips to drink at night, an excuse, "Got to take Tim to the rink," midnight to one, never mind when they had to be up in the morning. Oak would pound Coke and Gatorade and Mountain Dew. He took him in the mornings, too, often the very next morning, so that Oak was skating four or five times a week when he was eight. His father's hangovers must have been crushing at 5:00 a.m. But Oak would bug him until he'd do it.

When they let him skate, he scored. When he was eight, he might score six goals a game. He skated with the St. Ant's varsity in eighth grade. He had to fight half the team when Coach Coughlin's back was turned. He worked harder, got tougher. By eighth grade he was as big as they were. As a kid he couldn't sit still. Desks killed him. He wanted to move. He wanted to skate. Skating smoothed and focused his body and mind. And he liked to hit. It wasn't the violence, it was the challenge, body against body, mind on mind. The boom.

Oak sits on the Quincy rink benches. His hands shake all over the place. People are looking at him like he's nuts. If he had a mirror, he'd join them. Out on the ice, there's a little girl doing pirouettes. He really does suck in his breath as he jams his feet into the skates. It means nothing to him now, pain. Or it means so much he doesn't take note of it. Just one big fucking *ow*. Oxy does nothing for that, it only softens his body's memory of what it has been through so he can pretend to forget it and skate.

He stands on the blades. He feels okay. He stomps one foot to the mats, then the other. To wake them up. His eyes are good. He takes a breath. Blows it out. Another. He steps onto the ice.

He tells himself to take it easy. This is the first day since Albuquerque. The first day since the beatdown by the cops. The East Coast Hockey League is a big step back up, he skated the league in Carolina, and a big step back toward the AHL. He pushes from the boards. A couple kids with sticks swing by. The girl still spins at center ice, inside a ring of orange cones. He digs in and it's suddenly as if he's being branded from inside his skin. He circles back fast and clutches the boards. He presses his head to the glass.

There's a guy looking at him from the other side of the glass, standing there with his son. Oak shuts his eyes. He's tumbling. He opens them. Smacks the glass. The guy jumps back. Oak breathes in. He lifts his right knee high, then his left. He squats. Open his hips and back.

Oak shoves off again, does a slow pass along the boards so he can catch himself if he falls. This time, he feels stronger. He's still got no power, but he's upright, and his knees are working, and his hip is holding. He picks up speed. He arcs the corner, slides behind the net. That's where he makes his living. Anyone can skate free down the middle of the ice.

He picks it up a little more, coming at the blue line, a little more, leaning in, muscle memory and adrenaline, legs, hips, torso, shoulders, nuts, he wheels the far corner, feeling the turn. For a moment he sees the Worcester ice in his head, sees Rob Kellet watching approvingly from the ECHL team bench.

And then it's like he doesn't have a left hip. His left leg collapses, and he's in the air, and then he's slamming down across the ice, his body sliding, Oak bringing an arm up to protect his head, as he crashes into the base of the boards.

He lies there with his cheek on the ice. He tries to feel his hip.

He doesn't know if time has passed. He gets onto all fours. There's some blood. He wipes it from the ice with his sleeve.

Oak stands. He sets himself. He rolls his shoulders up, back, and down. He blinks away the lights that dance in front of his face. One breath. Two. He pushes out again and this time he pushes out hard, fuck this body and this boo-hoo collapse. And he is blue line, red line, blue line, storming the corner—and then he's falling again, the side of his head bouncing off the ice, his body hurtling into the boards.

He gathers himself again. He gets up. One skate has twisted off.

A kid in an orange vest skates over. "You all right, sir?"

Oak wipes his face.

"You need a hand?"

Oak tries to crush his foot back into the too-tight skate. The blade skids and he starts to fall again. The kid in the orange vest catches him, spins them toward the boards. They stand there side by side.

"Okay," Oak says, leaning carefully over to yank off his skate.

The kid puts an arm out. Oak takes it, lets himself be helped off the ice.

"Dude, you were flying," the kid says.

Oak sits back on a bench.

The girl at the counter comes over, gives him a towel. "Here," she says. She hands him his twelve dollars. "You should have this back."

He wants to say something to her. Her face is freckled, round, and kind. He wipes his own face, presses the towel to his forehead.

"You'll be all right," she says.

He holds the towel to his face, waits for her to go.

OAK GETS OUT INTO THE PARKING LOT. Kids and mothers are going in, the kids loaded up like they're going to war.

He feels like an idiot. He is an idiot. To be helped off the ice like charity.

He goes around to the back of the rink to piss. He's not going back inside.

Around the back, a group of kids, two Irish-white kids with their buzzcuts and hoodies, and a runt, Puerto Rican maybe, with a big fro of hair, are smoking a joint.

They palm it when Oak comes by, try to look tough.

"Give it here," Oak says.

"What?"

"The joint."

"You're no cop," one white kid says.

"Fuck off, man," the other white kid says.

He can tell the white kids are scared. The Puerto Rican kid is just watching.

"You look fucked up," the Puerto Rican kid says, staring at Oak.

Oak can't stand much longer on his hip.

"Give it here," Oak points at the kid with the joint, and the kid hands it over.

Oak fills his lungs with smoke, turns, unzips, and pisses against the wall. He exhales and takes another hit.

"Hey man—"

Oak tosses the joint into his piss.

"That's bullshit," the kid with the hair says. Oak thinks the kid's talking about the piss-wet joint until he turns to see the kid punch one of the white kids hard in the stomach.

"Hey—"

The kid with the hair tears into the other white kid, but they are big and dumb and twice his size and after a minute they've got the kid down on the ground and they're kicking him, the kid turtling, his quick hands racing back and forth from his skull to his ribs.

Oak roars, "HEY!"

But they're running, and he can't run after them. They're gone fast, giving him the finger, calling him a fat loser fuck.

Oak goes over to the kid with the hair.

"Get the fuck away from me."

"What was that about?"

"Go on, man. Get."

The kid struggles to his feet. There's gravel up in the blood in his big hair. His eyes start swimming.

"Sit down. Here—"

Oak gets an arm around the kid, the kid going woozy, sits him on the curb.

"How did you get here?"

"Jimmy's got a car."

"Jimmy one of those guys?"

"Yeah." The kid's bleeding through his shirt, bleeding from his head.

"Nice friends you got. How old are you?"

"Thirteen." When the kids says it, the kid looks at him with "Fuck You" in his eyes. He should put him in an ambulance.

"Let me look at your head."

"Fuck off."

But the kid says it scared. Oak spreads some of the kid's hair with his fingers to look at the gash. It's not deep. "I seen worse."

He has. He lifts the kid's shirt up. Pokes at the ribs with his fingers.

"Hey, shit man." The kid jumps. But he doesn't say anything more.

"You gotta eat more. Anyway, they're not busted. Let me see your eyes."

The kid looks at him. The kid's eyes are still swimming, but not as bad as they were.

"How much of that weed did you smoke?"

"I don't know."

"Any?"

"I don't really like the shit."

Oak takes the kid's face in one hand, turns his head one way, then the other.

He takes his hand away. There's blood on the boy's cheek, maybe the kid's, maybe his own. The boy wipes it. Looks at Oak.

"Who done *you* in?" the kid finally asks.

"Yeah . . . Where you live?"

"Not far."

"You got someone can come pick you up?"

"I can take a bus."

"I'm gonna put you in a cab."

"I don't got no money."

"Don't talk ghetto to me."

The kid looks at him.

"I got money," Oaks says. "I'll send you home. You got a phone?"

"No," the kid says fast. Then, "It's busted."

"Let's go." Oak gets him under the arms. Wraps a hand around the kid's bony shoulders and leads him, so he doesn't bolt to be found later facedown by the railroad tracks like the drunk his father once found who'd hit his head and froze there.

It takes them forever to get to the rink door. "Wait here," Oak tells him at the entrance.

The look again.

"You gonna wait?"

"Yeah."

"Yeah?"

He pushes open the door and finds the security guard.

"You good?" the guard says.

"Yeah. Listen. You got a phone? Mine's dead."

The guy looks at him, then gives him his cell. Oak walks over to the taxi list posted on the wall. Gets a cab. Brings the phone back to the guy. "Thanks."

Oak pushes back out the front doors. The kid is gone. He goes back around the corner. The kid's taking a leak against the wall.

"I didn't want to go back in there," the kid says.

"I know. Let's wait by the entrance. Let people think we beat the shit out of each other."

The kid doesn't smile.

They wait on the cab at the entrance.

"You play hockey?" the kid asks him.

"Yeah. You?"

"Nah. I'm a musician."

"Yeah? I'm a painter."

"No shit?"

"I'm painting a basement, you know?"

The kid smiles a little at that.

They stand and watch the cars, blowing cold breath into the air.

The taxi pulls in. Oak waves it down.

Oak opens the taxi door. When the kid tries to sit, he collapses, falls half against the open taxi door.

"What's up with that?" the driver says.

"He's all right. Just got knocked around on the ice."

Oak lifts the kid up, gets him into the seat.

Goes in and gets in the other side.

"You his father?"

"Tell him where we're going," Oak says.

"The point. Eighty-eight Dartmoor."

The driver glances at Oak in the mirror. Drives.

QUINCY CENTER HAS A LOT OF BANKS and bars and nice houses and, Oak remembers, a lot of hockey. You didn't have a lot of Puerto Ricans or whatever the kid is, not where Oak skated anyway. Then again, you didn't have a lot of guys from South Boston in El Paso, Texas.

The kid's got his eyes closed.

Oak pushes him. "Stay awake." The streetlights bounce along the window glass, off the kid's thin face.

"What's your name?" Oak asks.

"Kip. What's yours?"

"Oak."

"You don't know the kid's name?" the driver says. "What's going on?"

"I'm taking him home. I'm the responsible adult. So shut the fuck up."

Kip laughs and the driver turns up the radio and makes like they're no longer there.

Oak looks at the kid. "What kind of name is Kip?"

"I don't know. It's my name. From my mother. What kind of name is Oak?"

"It's short for something at least, O'Connor."

"Fuck off."

"Listen to yourself. You got a mouth. You kiss your mother?"

"My mother's dead." The kid says, his face in and out of shadow, his eyes white and brown, floating there.

"Mine too," Oak says.

Kip turns, looks out the window. The cabbie rolls through a light, past a liquor store and a garage, the streets looking tougher.

"You speak Spanish at least?"

"*You* speak Spanish?"

"*Poquito.*"

"You got a wife?" Kip asks, still looking out the window.

He can see Kip's face reflected in the window glass and he sees how young he is. He's like a stick. A stick with hair.

"No."

The radio goes into an ad for a vocational school.

"I got a kid," Oak says. "A daughter."

"How old?"

"About your age."

"Maybe you could hook us up, yo?"

Before he knows he's going to do it, he slaps the seat beside Kip, Kip jumping with the force. "Leave it."

The kid squeezes away from him, slowly, carefully, to the far side of the seat, turns from him again to the window.

Oak sees the cabbie looking at him in the rearview mirror. "I told you to drive," he says to the cabbie.

Kip's crying, lightly, trying not to. Oak's not sure what's going on. He looks at the blood on Kip's head and face.

"I'm sorry. It's just that . . . She and I, I don't see much of her, okay?"

"I was joking."

"I said I was sorry. Did you even hear what I fucking said?"

The cab turns off the avenue and pulls to the curb. "Okay," the driver says. "We're here. Out."

They're on a typical street, could be anywhere, could be Southie. Triple-deckers, brick apartments, road sand, parked cars and ice.

Kip gets out. Closes the door behind him.

Oak leans over. Reopens Kip's door. "Hey—"

Kip doesn't respond. Kip stands looking up at a run-down house.

"Kip—" He'd get out, but he knows the cab will take off if he does. "Make sure your father looks at that. You got to wash it, dump some peroxide on it. And don't go to sleep."

The taxi starts to pull away. "Hold on a minute," Oak tells the driver, but the driver keeps going. Oak watches Kip. Kip is standing in the dark, outside the house, the TV blue inside, not going in, staring, as the cab pulls away.

11

Oak rips open the ice bags, pours the ice into the cold bath water. He grips the edge of the tub. He takes a breath, steps into the bath, drops his body, immersing the slashes and the yellow-black bruises, the bones and joints. When his balls go under it's like being kicked. Oak blows the air out. Stay in, start the body over, get it back. His teeth are going now, his tongue jumping around in his mouth. He smacks the tub edge.

He skated like shit. Didn't even skate. Couldn't even skate. His spine caving, and his hip, his shoulder black again. He feels his heart jump around. He tries to steady it, steady everything, let his body try to heal. He's got five weeks before Worcester.

He's got three hundred bucks in the bank. He's going to have to see his Uncle Barry. His spine and his hip and his shoulder have made that clear. He can only just rip copper out of Catholic middle school walls.

When he first dislocated his shoulder, they taped it in place. It hurt like a motherfucker, like a Doberman sinking its teeth in over and over. But he played, not well, not long, but he showed them. In Michigan for the AHL. And in Wilmington, when he got knocked flat out, in the East Coast Hockey League, when the asshole Acey Green cross-checked him to the back of the head, he played later that very game. He just came to. He had no idea where the fuck he was. For the rest of that game he had no idea where the fuck he was, who they were playing, only that he *was* playing, and that he and Acey had to go. And that was going to be tricky. And then Kyler tried to do it for him, as soon as Oak hit the ice Kyler went for Acey, and Kyler and Acey went hard, there was blood, and the next day, feeling like he'd been hit by a semi, Oak had to pound the shit out of Kyler for showing him up, a twenty-three-year-old whose only chance was to be a goon, who Oak knew juiced in the summers, thinking he was going to out-goon Oak, when Oak wasn't even a goon at all.

LATER, HE GETS SOME BEER and sits in his sweats in his dead mother's armchair. He'll wait a little while, until he's cleaned up, to see Kate. Until the welt on his cheek is gone, the scab on his eyebrow, until he can walk without looking like Freddy Krueger.

He sent her postcards. He figures she got them. He should've done emailing, Facebook, Facetime. Game by bus by game, the days went away waiting on the nights.

He picks up his phone. Dials Major Tom. "Major, it's Oak."

"Oak—" Major sounds glad to hear from him. "How ya doing?"

"Pretty good."

"Yeah?"

Silence.

"You there, Major?"

The last beer's gone. Oak looks into the empty can, wipes

at his nose, looks out the window, the red lights of a jet cut through the sky.

"I skated today. Not bad," Oak lies.

"Good, Tim."

"Don't give my spot away. Yeah and I need my skates."

"Campbell's eager to have you back in January."

Mr. Campbell, the team owner, is the one who put his fights on the El Paso jumbotron, who got him the guest spot doing the local weather.

"What about you, Major? You eager?"

"Listen, Oak, Jill's sitting here beside me on the sofa. It's our movie night. You talk to that Kellet guy?"

"No," he lies again.

"I don't like him calling you."

"I used to skate for Kellet at PC."

"Why's he calling you now?"

"How the fuck should I know, Major?"

"I think it's because of Pat McDonald."

Oak feels the words like a slap. "He knows me from Providence, Tom," Oak says.

"I wasn't even going to tell you he called."

"I need my skates, Major. I meant to say that. Did I say that? Will you mail them to me? I'll text you my mother's address. I need them now. I'll pay you for the postage."

"I think your PC friend wants more of what happened to McDonald."

"Go back to your movie, Tom," Oak says, as steady as he can. "Tell Jill I say hi."

Oak hangs up. He knows Major is trying to look out for him. But he also knows Major is getting soft, that Major is content with his shit Texas job and his paving business. Oak knows that Rob Kellet will have film of his winning wraparound goal that Oak scored against Northeastern. It was a two pass give-and-go. Oak hit the point, then the goal crease, then he went behind the net for a be-tween-the-legs drop from his center that he tucked into the corner of the Huskie net. And Kellet will have his Beanpot Tournament end-to-end. That one made Boston TV. Kellet knows about Oak's start for Grand Rapids, Michigan, when Oak had ten points in ten games before his hip went out for the first time. The Gordie Howe hat tricks in Carolina, even if Carolina was down a league. The puck he took to the face when he blocked a goal in Jacksonville.

He's going to need Shark's gym. He's going to need Uncle Barry. He's going to need money to pay them both.

12

Oak goes up the three cement steps of Uncle Barry's apartment. A dog leaps against the inside of the door. Barry's got a South Boston Liberation Army sticker on the living room window. Oak doesn't want to be there. But he has to. He knocks. "Hold on," he hears from inside. It's Barry's voice. Oak hasn't seen his father's brother since he was a kid. They didn't visit Barry much, sometimes his father would go over. Oak's ma would have nothing to do with him.

"It's Tim," he hears himself say, "Timmy O'Connor."

"Fuck me, it isn't. *Go on*—" Barry yells at the dog, then, "Lauren!" and the barking comes from further back in the house.

The door opens. His uncle looks bad, like he should look, skinny, drug-collapsing face, gray stubble, green-dot tattoo, and black eye rings. But above the circles, inside them, are his uncle's still-bright blue eyes, piercing, like they cannot, will not, be diminished. Oak's always thought this, that his Uncle knows something, like his eyes have seen things, even though Barry's been a junkie and a kind of thug for as long as Oak has known him.

"You're fucking kidding me?" Barry's got his arm out through the door, reaching for him, pulling him into him, the door angled open at their side.

"Timmy, Jesus." Barry looks at him. "Jesus. Come on." Barry's got an arm around his neck and brings him inside, closing the door behind them. "Lauren—"

There's a woman there, maybe Oak's age, with dyed black hair and black clothes. She's wearing cowboy boots and hanging onto the pit bull. She's okay-looking, until she talks.

"Can I let Niamh go?" she asks.

"Yeah. Stand right there, Timmy. Let him come up to you. You're with me, so you're okay."

When she lets the dog go, it stands there, scared. It's pacing, shaking, growling. Suddenly, the dog charges at him, then stops, a game of chicken, to see if he'll flinch. He's going to stomp its fucking teeth in.

"Niamh," Barry says, low and cold. The dog comes up, cowers near Oak's hand. Oak scratches its ear.

"That's Lauren," Barry says, stepping into the front room that's surprisingly neat with a sofa and a chair and a coffee table. Irish prayer on the wall. Paintings of the ocean. A collage of a waterspout beneath planets and stars. Lauren gets the dog. Puts it in the kitchen. She goes back to the sofa.

"Timmy, shit. You want something? A beer?"

"I'm good."

"You back?"

He nods. "For a little bit. Maggie died."

"Oh, yeah? Shit. Shit. I thought I would have heard. Nobody told me. I saw her, not too long ago. In the Stop and Shop."

Oak nods.

"She looked good."

A cop siren runs down the street toward the water.

"You come home for her funeral?"

"Yeah."

"You still in, what is it, Providence?"

"Yeah."

"That's a nice place, Providence. Good place. Lauren, remember you and me went to Providence that time? We ate up on what-do-you-call-it? Federal Hill there."

"We met Buddy Cianci."

Barry smiles, the memory a photo developing. Oak knows the feeling. Pictures you forgot were in there.

"The mayor," Barry nods. "He tied some prick that was banging his wife to a chair and burned him with a cigarette."

"He was a real glad-hander to tell the truth," Lauren says. "When I told him I was from Wakefield he knew like nine people. From Wakefield."

He's standing there. The house smells bad. Dog shit and sweat. Lauren lights a cigarette. She coughs, bad, and the dog starts lunging against the kitchen door.

"NIAMH!" his uncle yells, and the dog and Lauren go quiet.

His uncle looks at him. They're both still standing in the middle of the room. The shades are down. His uncle's blue eyes narrow. They found Barry once bleeding behind Tynan Elementary. Someone called Oak's father. Barry was slashed right across his chest, as a message.

"I'm guessing this is more than a social call, Timmy."

Oak knows he needs to show his uncle respect. He doesn't deserve it, but Oak came to him, to his house. When Oak was four and Arlene six, Uncle Barry got a boat. They rode around Boston Harbor. His father brought sandwiches. They watched the sun go down and they watched the stars. Barry taught them to sing "All God's Creatures Got a Place in the Choir". He told good jokes.

"I don't know if this is something you can help me with, Barry."

On the sofa, Lauren's nodding off, the lit cigarette hanging between her fingers, down by her knee.

"I don't know if . . . this is anything you might be able to do. So excuse me for any mistake."

"Okay."

"My hip is blown. My low back is fucked. My shoulder. I mean, you can look at me. I'm pretty down, Barry. I need some help."

"Sit down, Tim."

"I'm good."

This pisses his uncle off a little.

"I need," Oak says it quickly, "if you have it for some reason, some Oxy."

"Oxy?" His uncle glances at Lauren.

"Probably like everything you've got. Everything you can spare. Adderall, too. Roxy, Dexy."

"I don't spare anything, Tim."

Lauren laughs.

"I'm not asking as a favor, Barry."

Oak looks at his uncle steady, to remind him that he's not a child, they're not on a boat, he's not punching out Gold Glove bets, that Catholic respect is long gone.

"I probably have something, Tim. Lauren?"

"We've got like fifteen 40s.

A week of skating if he's careful with it.

"OC, Tim." His uncle's eyes shimmer. "Not the coated shit."

"You got 80s?"

"My nephew . . ." Barry grins in Lauren's direction. "Nothing like that. And we've been saving these for a special occasion. OC, Timmy. Four hundred bucks. Family rate."

"I've got two hundred."

"I'll give you eight then. And a couple lid poppers."

Oak nods. That will last him for three days.

Lauren goes into the kitchen. When she closes the door so the dog doesn't get out, the bad smell comes at him like a fog.

"We should get a beer, Timmy. We've never been close, I know that, but we're older now. I'm fucking sixty. Can you believe it?"

Oak smiles as best he can.

"Hey, Timmy. Hold on."

His uncle opens the drawer of the TV console. Inside, there's a row of VHS boxes. And a gun. The gun is squat, snubbed. Oak saw plenty of guns in Texas, usually half-concealed on cocky rednecks. A gun in Barry's drawer is a lot more menacing. Barry gets a VHS box. Closes the console drawer. Oak wonders if Barry wanted him to see the gun or not. His uncle opens the VHS box and inside there are little bags of powder. Coke or smack or crystal. He's guessing it's smack.

"Better than Oxy. And a quarter the price. You done it yet?"

"No."

"Take it," his Uncle presses the little envelope of heroin into his hand. "I got more."

"Okay," Lauren says, coming back though the kitchen door. She's got a baggie with his pills.

13

The building site's not far from the red line so at lunch Oak takes the T to Quincy Center and gets on a bus to the kid's street. To make sure the kid hasn't gone loopy from a concussion, to make sure he's okay.

The porch light is still on in the daytime. What's left of the yard patch is bad: brown grass and dirt. It's Friday, so Kip's probably, hopefully, at school. Oak just wants to know, to hear how he is. He knocks on the door. He's got paint all over him. Knocks once more. He can see a light on and now, listening, he can hear a TV. Knocks again, harder. He doesn't ring the buzzer. He's always hated them, even as a kid they made him jump.

Someone's coming and the door opens narrow, and there's a skinny guy, greasy-haired and smoking.

"Yeah?"

He can smell the booze and smoke oozing out of Kip's father.

"I brought your kid back. Yesterday."

The guy doesn't say anything.

"I'm checking to see if he's all right."

"Why wouldn't he be?"

Oak looks at Kip's father. He could knock the skinny dude into tomorrow. He looks past him into the house. There's no woman involved, he can see that. Only this unemployed asshole.

He remembers that Kip's mother is dead. He feels his anger soften.

"Yeah. Okay. Good."

Oak sticks his hand out for some reason. The guy takes it. "He's a good kid," Oak says.

"Okay," Kip's father says. The guy's hand is ice.

Oak walks back toward the street, Kip's father's eyes knocking at his back.

14

The second-floor piping and wiring are as easily ripped out as those in the basement. Oak's got an escape plan in his head in case he needs it. Out the first-floor window in the back, then down the hill through what used to be the playground to the street below. Slats is wiping brick dust from his face with a rag.

"It's chickenshit, Slats. What's really going on?" Oak bundles wire. "Why isn't Only here?"

"It's four hundred bucks, Oak. Easy."

"How do you know him?"

"I don't. Zinky does."

Slats tosses the rag to the floor. Oak drags his ladder down the hallway, the hallway still lined with school lockers.

"You think—"

"What?"

"Nothing." Oak knows it's not his right to say it. But it is. Farther down the hall, Esteban and Jorge are joking as they strip thick wires from the wall. "You think this is being a good role model?"

Slats's face goes hard and Oak doesn't blame him. "Are you fucking kidding me, Oak?"

"Never mind. I'm sorry."

"Because Catholic school costs money, Oak, and you don't want, I don't want my kids going to public." Slats looks at him. "Do you, Oak?"

"No."

"No, I didn't think so. Although, really, I got no way of knowing."

"Let's leave it alone."

"Yeah." Slats picks up his wrench.

"When I get cleaned up, I'm gonna come by."

"This comes with the job, Oak. Unless you got a way for me to make money."

"I know it. I know it does, Slats. I'm sorry."

Slats is holding the wrench at the end of his arm. Oak sees the scar Slats has on his nose from where Slats's old man Great Santini'd it shooting hoops.

Ivan comes up the stairs, tells the Mexican guys to work faster.

"You come back to town," Slats says quietly, like he's wanted to say it for a while. "You think everything is going to be all right. Like it was. Like we're fifteen. We're not fifteen anymore, Oak."

"Slats—"

"Kate's fourteen. You want to come back, hockey star, kiss and make up? Tell her how you were on TV? Why don't you make a fucking move on Shannon, too, while you're at it? Why don't you tell Kate what you were doing on her birthdays? What you were doing when she was four and six and ten, when she was crying in the middle of the nights for no reason? I know what I was doing then. I know what Shannon was doing. We were with Kate."

"I'm not paying you to talk," Ivan says. He spits into a dust covered water fountain. "Or to take two-hour lunches."

"Why don't you fucking lift a hammer?" Oak says, looking at Ivan's fat nose, thinking he could bend it back in place.

"That's why I have you."

15

Oak wakes in his mother's armchair. Sometimes he can sleep if his body is upright. In Texas, in Florida, he slept in the movies during matinees. The sun's coming up. He gets out of the armchair. He goes up the stairs before his body catches up with his brain. In his room, he gets an OC from inside the zipped pocket of his duffel bag. He grabs a plastic puck that looks clean enough from the shelves near his bed. He sets the pill on his bureau, rolls the puck over the OC, crushing it. He wets his finger and gets what's on the puck into his mouth. His brain fires in anticipation. His body knows what's coming, the small relief that will let him go to Shark's gym and lift and bike and then, soon, skate. He rails the Oxy with a dry finger, leans over the line, and sucks it up his nose. He shuts his eyes. Opens them. He looks at the guy looking back at him in the bureau's mirror. Looks out the window to the street. He's got eleven pills left.

He goes into his mother's bedroom. It looks the same. Her bed. Her bureau. Her closet's open and her robe still hangs on the door. There are a couple photos of him as a kid on her bureau and a bunch of Arlene and Arlene's children. The kids are skating, sledding, swimming. There's a professional-looking photo of Arlene and her husband and her boys with Buzz Lightyear at Disney World. He looks at himself. He's in a suit for Auntie Ciara's second wedding. He's seven. In the other, he's littler, standing in the water with his sister, smiling. And there's a two-picture frame of him and Arlene in their high school graduation gowns.

He finds a shoebox of hockey stuff on a shelf in her closet. Her clothes still hang there. She mostly wore jeans. Her shoes. He takes the box and puts it on her bureau. There are all the clippings, the team photos, the championship photos and the MVP photos and a couple of him boxing. There he is at nine when he knocked the kid over the ropes. At eleven when he scored six goals in a game. St. Anthony Varsity MVP in tenth grade. Catholic Conference MVP in eleventh and twelfth grade. And there he is on his mother's bureau mirror, as a baby, she's holding him in her arms. He's in a bib that reads "Lock Up Your Daughters." His father probably took the picture. She's grinning. She looks young and happy.

There's a knocking downstairs at the front door.

He waits it out. He's not sure it's real. It comes again. Then the bell.

Arlene must have forgotten her keys, he's guessing. He doesn't know what time it is. He finds his phone. It's seven in the morning.

Oak takes the stairs one step at a time. Even railing it, the Oxy takes time, comes on first with an itching across his skin. At the foot of the stairs he squats, pushes back up. He's okay. He slaps the wall. He's not done and he's not going to be done. He's going to skate for Rob Kellet, and get back to where he belongs.

"Jesus, Arlene—" He gets the front door open.

Kip is standing there, alone on the steps, a wintry sun silver behind him.

Seeing Oak, the kid starts away, backing down the steps and turning like he's going to run.

"Hey—" Oak calls after him.

Kip is wearing the same blue hoodie. There's a blood stain on the back of it. Kip turns and he's like a dog, Oak thinks, he wants to come up the steps but isn't sure.

"What are you doing?" Oak says.

"Nothing. I—" and then Kip says nothing.

Oak squints into the sun. "How did you know where I live?"

"I don't know."

"You want to come in?"

Kip walks up their steps and stands in their front hall.

Oak didn't realize how bad the kids beat him: Kip's eye is welted, his hands are torn up. Kip's looking around. Oak looks around, too. For some reason, Oak feels embarrassed in front of the kid, the empty bottles of beer around his mother's chair, his clothes thrown on a table.

"Someone must've come in the middle of the night, made this mess . . ."

Kip doesn't say anything.

"That was a joke."

Kip doesn't say anything.

"You want a drink or something? I probably only got water. I'd give you a beer, but it's too early in the day, even for a man like yourself."

Still nothing.

"Okay," Oak says. "Well, I was just taking off."

"I saw you."

He doesn't know what Kip means.

"You don't need to come by."

"What?"

"You don't need to come by. That's what I came to say. You're just a guy who pisses on a building. You're shit."

Kip turns and leaves, leaving the front door open.

Oak watches him go, Kip's hoodie up, a black dot into the cold sun.

16

Shark's gym hasn't changed from the outside: the black silhouettes of two boxers on the red sign, the barred storefront windows. The gym is on the Dorchester side of the expressway, near Upham's Corner, there's some flowerpots and bike racks now, a Dunkin' Donuts and a Vietnamese takeaway. Oak rode his bike like hell when he left after dark as a kid.

Shark's got a camera now over the red metal door, but it's open, and inside the gym looks the same, busy, like it's doing pretty good: the four bags, the ring, the floor ring, the bikes and weights and the fluorescent lights hanging down.

Oak steps inside. He breathes in the hot adrenal. One-two hook. The first time Oak landed a hook he sent a guy four years older than him into Shark's office carried by two trainers. After the second time, Shark started to teach him himself.

Oak looks around. A couple firefighter guys are going at it, his age, he doesn't recognize them. On the bags, some younger guys who look like maybe they could go. Two kids are grappling, surrounded by a bunch of other kids, some kind of mixed martial arts, their kid trainer straddling a bag that should be hanging. At the heavy bag, a fat kid sweats out weak punches, his track-suited father urging him on.

It makes sense, that kids would want MMA more than boxing, he thinks. He'd probably been the same. He likes it okay. Shark won't though. There's no way Shark wants that in his gym, but Oak figures that MMA pays the rent for those kids who want to learn to hit. Like he did. It's a good sport, boxing. Shark used to say you punch from the *earth*.

He knows he's stalling. The fluorescents are fucking with the soft places in the back of his eyes but he's not going to go into Shark's office wearing shades. He sees Shark at his desk, the same desk, unwrapping a breakfast sandwich. Shark's big eyeglasses slip down his nose. His office has never had a door. Behind Shark are the photos of Marvelous Marvin, of Bernie Hopkins, Shark's Wall of Fame. Oak's up there somewhere. And beside it, the carefully chosen Temporary Wall of Shame. Oak was up there a couple times. Shark should be in a movie. Black guy, runs a boxing gym on the edge of Southie. Morgan Freeman. Except in the movies they don't talk about forty hours working at the T. About working weekends, so that you're working seventy hours. And the kids and the parents and the fighters come and go, the firemen and cops retired at forty-five, and then you're old. In the movies, the gym runs itself, with a little whiskey for the black man, a few stories about his glory days when he lost on a technicality to Cassius Clay.

The movies never, ever talk about the grind. Oak doesn't blame them. Who wants to see that for ten bucks? The best boxing movie he ever saw was *The Champion*. The worst is the one with Clint Eastwood and the girl. Total bullshit. In the movies, Shark would die just as Oak is making his big comeback in the ring. In the movies, no one in Southie goes to college.

He goes into Shark's office.

Shark looks up from his sandwich. "Hello, Oak."

"I'm sorry. About the church. About the funeral." He can't really meet his old coach's eyes, with how he is, with the Oxy opening inside him.

Around him, Oak sees the familiar photos and the trophies, the three round cards on the wall: thirteen, fourteen, fifteen. A reminder, Oak can hear Shark's voice in his head even as he's standing there in front of him, that fights used to go fifteen rounds not twelve. For the Irish crybabies and the wannabe rappers. Fifteen rounds.

"I need to work out." He just says it, because it's true.

On a shelf, there's a photo of Shark's daughter, Angie, when she was young, holding a red glove to her father's chin, Shark mooning a face. There's toy subway cars. A serenity prayer in needlepoint. Shark with the featherweight he took to Germany, Shark and the welterweight he took to the Mirage. Oak closes his eyes.

"Hey. Tim." Shark snaps his fingers in front of Oak's face.

Shark is looking at him with that long look that gets inside Oak, Shark's right eye drooping from a punch Shark took as a boy, deadening the nerve in his eyelid. *You dropped your glove? You didn't run your hills? You talked shit about an opponent?* That long look.

"You can work out here, Oak, as long as you don't smell of liquor. You got any money to pay?"

"No."

"You can clean up nights. Work out then. I'll get you keys. Save my back."

"I was thinking maybe I could work out now."

"Nights."

"I got a tryout in a month."

Shark goes back to his sandwich. "Nights."

There's nothing to do but go. He's wasted an OC. He'll run the Sugar Bowl around the harbor when he gets home, maybe see if his old rollerblades still fit.

"And introduce yourself to John Morton and his son JJ on the way out. They've got keys, so you'll be seeing them."

Keys mean John is paying premium to come in when he likes.

Oak walks out of Shark's office. He heads over to the guy in the track suit and his soft-looking son.

"I'm Tim O'Connor," Oak says.

"I know it." John Morton sticks his hand out. "I was a senior at St. Ant's when you were a freshman."

Oak shakes John's hand. He has no idea who the guy is.

"This is my son, JJ. This is Mr. O'Connor. He was a helluva a hockey player."

Oak shakes the kid's hand. JJ's big, sloppy, sweating, with a buzz cut like his father's.

"You still skating?" John asks. Oak sees the guy taking him in now, like the guy's eyes are focusing and finally able to see what his fellow alum has become.

Oak nods. John keeps eyeing him in a way that Oak doesn't like.

"JJ plays hockey," John says.

"I'm not very good," the son says.

"You enjoy it?" Oak asks the kid.

"What?"

"You like skating?"

"Yeah." He can tell the kid doesn't.

"We're sort of looking for a new coach," John says. "Over at

St. Cathy's. For the girls' team. I teach there now." Oak sees the guy kind of look him over, deciding on how he should feel about what he is seeing.

"You went over to the enemy," Oak says. They used to dominate St. Cathy's which had a small program and skated in the basement of the Catholic League.

"The enemy had the job." John laughs. "That's why I come in here. To remember how it was." John turns to his son. "I saw this guy score twice against Harvard. Those assholes."

JJ laughs.

"Anyway, the coach we've got, you ever hear of him? Nick Duffy? Skated for Lowell. Nice guy. Too nice. English teacher. Sucks as a coach."

"Don't know him."

"You get in an accident or something, Oak?"

"Yeah." Oak looks down at the son, JJ, and points over at two teenagers who are sparring in the ring. "See the bigger kid's legs there?" Oak says to JJ. "They're dead. Watch the smaller kid. He can fight. Sports car beats a truck. Remember that. Shark says that."

"But you're a truck."

The big kid stumbles in the ring, and the smaller kid side-shuffles and clocks him to the mat.

17

Oak goes into Donahue's bar at ten o'clock on a Saturday with the envelope of photographs for Joan Linney. He glances around. Joan is not there. He's both relieved and disappointed not to see her in the bar, with her coffee, with whatever business she was doing in her mind. He orders a beer.

It's the same bartender as before. "You guys selling this place?"

"You buying?"

"I wish." He pays the guy.

He takes the beer to a table. Gets himself into the chair.

He doesn't sleep at night anyway. He'll clean up Shark's gym then work out. When his hip and shoulder are better, he'll skate again. He's got a month before the Worcester tryout. Joan wanted him to draw up a list of names of people in town who might write something on his behalf. He doesn't want to get into that. He saw the look of disappointment on Shark's face. He's not in any kind of shape to ask anyone to tell her how great he is, even if he could find someone willing to do it.

He steadies himself with the beer. He takes a blank sheet of paper from the envelope and gets the pen that he brought from his jacket pocket. The first name he writes down is Rob Kellet of PC. And then Major. He writes down the St. Ant's coach, Coach Coughlin, but he doesn't know where he lives or even if he is living. He writes down the name of the guy who ran the skate club at Murphy's Rink but knows he's dead but maybe his wife would remember Oak. He looks at the piece of paper. He can't remember the names of anyone else.

The bar door opens. Two suits come in. One guy orders a shot. They look like brokers. One of the guys could be a cop. The guy drinks the shot and pays. The guy gets his change back. Oak sees him hand a small baggie to his friend who quickly stuffs it in his overcoat pocket. Oak remembers the guy in the men's room, thumping his head against the wall. He drains the beer and gets out of the place.

JOAN'S LOOKING AT THE PHOTOS, sitting at the public defender office desk. "How old are you here?" In the photo, Oak's leaning on the net in Murphy's Rink, grinning.

He looks at it. "Nine I guess."

"You look like a teenager."

"That's when I started growing. That's probably why I'm smiling."

The Paul Newman lawyer is watching them, drinking coffee from a mug.

"And here?" It's a team photo for the St. Ant varsity, when he first skated with them in eighth grade.

"Fourteen. I couldn't play in the actual games until the next year. I don't know why my mother kept it."

"Does she have photos all over the house?" She smiles.

"Nah." It occurs to him then that she didn't. She did back when he was in high school. In college maybe. "To tell you the truth. It embarrasses me to look at that stuff."

"May I keep this for a bit?"

"Yeah. Sure. You can have it."

"And did you draw up a list of names."

He shakes his head. "No."

"Okay." She labels the envelope Tim O'Connor Boyhood.

"I want to apologize," he says. "For the other day. For being a dick."

He notices how heavy her lids are, like she can only just keep her eyes from closing into sleep.

"Thank you," she says. Her chin drops. She blanks out, only for a second, sitting there at her desk. Oak looks to see if the other lawyer sees it. The guy does. The guy looks at Oak like he could strangle Oak for seeing it too.

Joan shakes her head and looks up. Her eyes water. She wipes them. She doesn't seem to know that she's been out. Or if she does know, she hides it. "I'll be in touch soon, Tim," she says.

"How's the painting going?"

She's quiet. "Not very good."

"I can do it for you. I got experience. Me and another guy. A kid, actually." As a kid one summer he painted houses on Cape Cod, stayed with his grandmother in Bourne, skated in Falmouth with a mess of hard-throwing Murphys. "You and your husband can trust me," he quickly adds. "I mean, if you can't trust a guy who pops a cop, who can you trust?"

Her laugh jumps from her. "You and your partner work weekends?"

The lawyer guy stands up from his desk. "Joan this is not a good idea."

Oak ignores him. "That's our specialty. And we don't charge double for weekend work. Only time-and-a-half." Her smile lifts him. "You don't have to pay me. Maybe you could pay the kid something. We can start next weekend. You can fire the other guys. Give me your address."

Joan sinks back in her chair, away from him.

"Joan," the other lawyer says.

Oak turns and looks at the guy. "Your house need work too?"

The lawyer returns his gaze. "Okay, buddy," the guy says.

Her voice is steady. "I could use some help." She's talking like the guy at the other desk is not even there. But it's not really to him, either. She's talking to a place that does not quite reach him. Oak has to step into it, like he can watch what she is saying land. She writes her address on a piece of paper. "Ten o'clock next Sunday?" she says. "Or do you go to church? My sister still goes. Maybe the boy does?"

"I got the supplies," he lies.

"They're not stolen, are they?"

"Yes."

Joan smiles again. She stands. He feels a kind of warm wave. He moves into it carefully, so as not to flatten it, and takes the address from her.

"Okay, Tim. Don't come to my house if you've been drinking." She walks past him and out into the small waiting room. He feels the pull of the wake of her. He has to stop himself from turning to watch her as she goes.

"She told me about you." The other lawyer says. "Tough guy. Beats up a cop. A cop with a baby at home."

"You don't know what you're talking about."

"I know a punk when I see one." The lawyer stands up. He's big, with thick white hair and a booze-lined nose.

Oak senses the heavy righteousness in the guy. The guy's got jam, white hair or not, red nose or not. "Okay," Oak nods. "I got it." The guy's looking out for her. "I hear you," Oak says, to give the guy respect. He sees the guy relax a little.

Joan comes back in with a skinny, stupid-looking black guy, and Oak knows what that guy's seeing, a big, stupid-looking white guy, so he nods at the guy, the legion of the dumb, and the guy nods back, and Joan's eyes are on his as Oak puts her number deep into his pants pocket so it won't get lost or thrown away.

18

On the last day of the job, after sundown, Oak and Esteban are on the school roof, tearing the copper gutters off, while Slats and Jorge are in the back of the school stripping copper from the HVAC. Ivan's in his truck with the heat running. Tom Zink's on his phone on the school steps. It's dark and cold. His hands are working and his shoulder is working, but it's like there's sand in his joints, and he can't stop the shakes. Esteban's pounding at the gutter joint with a hammer to loosen it when the joint snaps suddenly and Esteban lurches, his leg sliding over the lip of the icy roof.

Below him, Oak sees Tom Zink running.

Behind Zink, Oak sees Slats tearing across the lawn away into darkness.

It's like Oak's watching it on TV. Two figures, disappearing, leaving a soft blanket of darkness. And then he wakes up. Two cop cars careen onto the site, lights flashing, sirenless.

"Move it—" Oak shouts out to Esteban, and Oak's down the school stairs, fast along the hallway, rolling himself out the back window to the lawn, sliding, cop lights slashing, getting to his feet, running the shadow's edge toward the woods, the path he's made in his mind, a cop car speeding across the parking lot, Ivan caught in a flood of lights.

Running down the hill, falling forward, there's no footing, when Oak reaches the bottom, he's hurled along the sidewalk. He gets his forearms up. He slides and scrapes across the gravel and ice, smacking against a mailbox.

And then he sees the beam of a flashlight and a cop is coming through the woods, down the path, at him. Oak gets to his feet. He's not going to be able to outrun the guy. He hustles down the sidewalk. Past Vietnamese takeout joints, he's trying to remember the road to the T station. He turns quickly to see the cop walking fast down the road behind him. Oak crosses the street, hoping he's on the way to the station, so he can say he's on the way to the station. He's going to fucking kill Slats, he can't have more trouble, he should have known Slats would fuck it up. He doesn't want to look over his shoulder again, but he does and he sees the cop hurrying across the street. There's a package store on the next corner, with some kids hanging around outside. The cop's on his radio, Oak can hear it, the cop is gaining on him from behind. Oak makes it to the packie.

"Buy us something, will ya? I got money," one of the kids says standing under a flashing sign for Miller Lite. For a second, Oak sees Kip lying on the ground behind the rink, standing in his hoodie at his front door.

Oak looks back up the sidewalk. The cop's talking at two Vietnamese guys, the Vietnamese guys looking at the ground. Oak gets inside the liquor store.

Inside it's old Savin Hill: a Jimmy Fund football pool, construction paper turkeys with kids' names scrawled across the tails, a neighborhood guy working the register. Oak makes like he's looking around.

"You need something?" the guy behind the counter asks.

"I'm good."

"Getting cold." White guy, fifties, Popeye Doyle.

"Freezing." Oak gets a fifth of JD.

"Good for the Miami game though," the guy says.

Oak nods. "Squish the fish."

The guy laughs. Oak puts the bottle on the counter.

The cop comes into the store. Looks around. Oak's the only customer.

"Can I help you?" the cashier says to the cop who's black.

"You know this guy?" the cop says, pointing at Oak.

"Sure."

The cop nods. "Anyone else come in here? Mexican guy maybe? Or a guy looks like he's been running?"

The cashier looks at Oak again. Oak can feel the sweat on his forehead, the sweat rolling down inside his arms. The cashier puts his bottle in a bag. Oak tries to get his wallet from his pants pocket. Sees the grease on his sweats, the plaster dust on his boots. His fingers are stiff, his knuckles are slow. The cop sees it. The cashier sees it. Oak hands the cashier two twenties. His busted hands shake like those of a shaky-handed drunk.

"What are you doing here?" the cop says to Oak.

Oak draws a breath in slow, lets it go slower. He looks at the cop. "Drinking."

The guy behind the counter laughs. The cop takes a step toward him.

"My grandfather lives here."

"Where?" the cop says fast. Oak keeps his face neutral, doesn't look away from the cop. He hopes his photo is not taped to the dashboards of every squad car within fifty miles of Dorchester Heights. "G Street," he says. "You want to meet him?"

The cop points at him. "You got a mouth." And turns to leave.

The cashier calls after the cop. "If you want to do something useful, get rid of those rats on my doorstep, will you, officer? That'd be something good."

The cop is gone.

"Guy's not even from around here," the cashier says, shaking his head. "Who's your grandfather anyway?"

"John O'Connor. But he's dead."

"I'll look out for him," the guy says, pointing up to the sky.

19

Oak's breathing. In the quiet and the dark against the whirl in his head, inside the dark throb in his bones. On the floor of his boyhood room. The only light in the room is from the streetlamp. He hung a blanket to try to block the light that creeps in around the shade. Above him on the walls, his boyhood posters: Cam Neely, Ray Borque, Probert, Terry O'Reilly, the Brawl Street Gang. Eminem. The trophies: bantam champs, peewee champs, St. Ant's champs, the silver mittens. MVP. MVP. MVP. The headlines from *The Herald* and *The Ledger* that his mother framed and hung in his room.

He hears someone outside listening through his bedroom window. He's stuck on the floor but he can hear them, there's two of them now and they're talking, and then he wakes up more and knows there's no one outside his second-story window in the Southie night, but he can sense them now down the street, in a car, listening in as he spins in the dark. And the spinning gets worse and Oak grips the floor, rolls over, and sits. He gets his head into his hands. He holds it against the rush of sick building in his guts.

20

Oak's driving Arlene's Voyager down to Quincy at eight in the morning before heading west to Joan's house. Arlene lent him the car because Kyle was going to New Jersey for two weeks. A two-car family. Oak doesn't want to drive his ma's car. He's sweating. He's hoping he doesn't stink, arriving there, busted-up, stinking. He bought a new shirt at a place on Broadway. He makes a left at a big Catholic church that's done up for Christmas and then down past a mosque that isn't and finds Kip's house with the shitty mud-frozen lawn.

He knocks on the door. Nothing. Rings the bell a few times despite himself.

He went to Home Depot and bought all the shit he could have stolen from the Russian Georgians if Slats hadn't somehow fucked it up.

Kip answers the door. He looks like he hasn't slept. He has dark patches under his eyes. Dracula meets Frankenstein. Kip stares back at him.

"Where's your father?"

"He's not home."

"What are you doing?"

"Standing here."

There're record albums all over the living room. Oak didn't notice that before. There are shelves in the living room filled with them that stack up to the ceiling.

"You want to make some money?"

"No."

"All right."

Fuck him, Oak thinks.

Then feet hit the floor upstairs. Someone's home.

"Okay," Kips says quickly. Kip pulls on a sweatshirt and sneakers and is out the door, pushing past him. Oak checks back over his shoulder, back at the empty house with the records up the walls. He doesn't see Kip's father.

Kip gets in the front seat of Arlene's car.

"You want a doughnut?"

He got a bag of doughnuts.

"No."

"You eat anything?"

Kip doesn't say anything more, just looks out the passenger window.

"Go ahead." Oak puts the bag in Kip's lap.

Kip takes out a cruller. "Thanks."

The kid's hair sticks up all over the place. "You got serious salad," Oak says.

"Salad?"

"Hair."

OAK FINDS JOAN'S HOUSE, an old Victorian, in Brookline, a half-hour away from Southie in a posh neighborhood behind BC. The College. Oak betrayed Boston College, all of Boston and Ireland, by going to the lesser Catholics at PC. BC betrayed him by not offering good money. He beat their asses twice that season and twice the next for good measure. Once, when he lamped a guy in the corner at BC's Kelley Rink, he looked up and was face-to-face with Teddy Kennedy. The senator sipped his beer.

He parks in Joan's driveway. It's a real house—lawyer money. Two lawyers probably, he doesn't know what her BC-loving husband does. The Voyager bumps over a crack in the driveway. He can fix that, Oak thinks. He spent a summer pouring tar when he skated in Florida.

"She your girlfriend?" Kip hasn't spoken the whole ride. They just played the radio.

"She's our boss. Your job is to shut up and paint."

They get out of the car. Kip stands there, on the other side of the car, looking up at the house.

"Come on," Oak says. "You got as much right as she does to be here. In this neighborhood." Oak slams the car door. "To be anywhere."

A trellis along the front walk lies on its side, collapsed.

"Her grape arbor's messed up," Kip says.

"Her grape arbor?"

"Yeah. See?" Kip lifts up the browning vines. "Grape leaves."

They get up her front steps. "And she needs a Christmas wreath," Kip says looking at her barren yellow door. "It's November already."

Joan's at the door before he can knock. She's not smiling, but she's not not smiling. She's in a long black shirt, a man's shirt. Sweatpants and bare feet. Her sleeves are rolled up. Oak notices her slender wrists, the way her face lifts him even when her dark eyes quickly look away. Maybe they woke her. Maybe, he's thinking, she doesn't sleep.

"I made a mistake, Tim," she says to the space between him and Kip.

"We got all the stuff."

"I'm sorry."

He's standing on the steps.

"Your arbor."

She looks at him.

"Sorry, I mean we noticed it."

"It doesn't matter," she says. He can only just hear her.

"I know. I don't know why I said it."

Kip's still standing behind him on the wet lawn. Oak jerks his head at him. Kip comes up the front steps. "This is my director of operations, Kip. Kip, this is our boss, Mrs. Linney."

Inside, Oak sees that the house is filled with art and books. There are running shoes, his and hers, on a mat by the door.

Feeling like he's got no good place to put his hands, he shoves them into the pockets of his sweats. It's like he's stepping into something, something delicate, not the house, not even her exactly. He waits for the husband to come down the stairs. He imagines a bookish guy, a skinny runner.

"Hi," Kip says, out of nowhere. "I'm director of operations."

Joan smiles suddenly. "Hi."

She looks at Oak.

"He stole the car," Oak says.

She smiles again, shakes her head a little. "Okay. Come on."

They follow her inside. She leads them into the small dining room that looks out to a fenced backyard. An antique-looking glass chandelier hangs from the ceiling. The dining room table is covered in a drop cloth, newspapers cover the floor. Three of the walls are yellow. The fourth, the one with the window to the yard, is slashed with maroon colored paint, like someone took a brush and used it as a knife. The newspaper at the baseboard is splattered in red.

Oak turns his body away from the wall. He feels how his mind is going to show him McDonald's bleeding face and he stuffs it, the image sticking in his heart that starts to pound. He's going to make a joke, about a monkey painting the wall, but the way she's standing there, just outside of the room, in the kitchen, looking in, looking embarrassed, ashamed even, stops him.

"I've got a lot of work to do," she says. She doesn't look at them. "So, I'll leave you two."

"You need primer," Oak says. "With this kind of paint."

She nods. "I didn't know."

"I brought some," Oak says. "Enough for this room, but the others—"

"We can just do that then," she says. "This room."

"Okay." He nods at her.

"Okay," Joan says.

Kip walks around him into the room.

Oak and Kip get the rollers and the brushes and the drop clothes and the primer from the car. She's got enough paint and a ladder. Oak gathers all the newspapers from the dining room floor and balls them into the corner. Gets the drop cloths down.

"You ever paint before?" he asks Kip.

"Sure."

Oak looks at him.

"No."

Oak nods. "It's simple." Oak gets the top off the primer, stirs it. "You stir it, pour it in the fucking pan." Oak pours. "Then here, grab a roller—"

Kip picks up a roller. It's twice as long as him and it swings past the chandelier.

Oak points at the pan. "You don't want too much on the roller. Just sort of get it in there."

Kip pushes the roller into the pan. Primer slops out over the sides of the pan. Kip jumps back. "Oh shit, sorry—" Kip stares at the spilled primer, like he's broken a vase or something. He keeps staring at it.

Oak's not sure, for a minute, what's up. "That's why we've got the drop cloth," Oak says. "Here, look—" Oak eases his own roller into the pan. "You just sort of coat the roller. Okay? Turn and roll it on the wall. It ain't brain surgery."

Kip lowers his roller carefully into the pan. Kip gets his roller onto the wall. They prime there, side by side.

"Welcome to the working world," Oak says.

WHEN THEY GET THE FIRST WALL DONE, Oak goes into the kitchen to see if there's a radio. Kip hasn't said a word, but he's holding up his end. Joan has stayed upstairs. The husband's still out. They've got a Bose radio next to the coffee maker.

There are pictures, too, and there's the husband: brainy-looking as he figured, glasses, marathon-fit. There are pictures of them in what looks like Texas, maybe Arizona, but it looks like Texas. Matching sun hats. Matching water bottles. Joan on a bicycle, smiling. Joan swimming in a lake, in a red swimsuit, her legs and arms and face shining in the sun.

Oak looks away from the photos. He just wants to paint their house. Her house. He hopes he never sees the guy. The guy that should be doing this himself.

He unplugs the radio and carries it into the dining room, the cord dangling to the floor. He looks around.

"What the fuck are we doing here, Kip?" he says.

"Painting," Kip says.

"Yeah." Oak smiles. He plugs the thing in. Kip gets up on the ladder to tape the second wall like Oak showed him. Kip's shirt rides up. Oak sees again the beatdown the kids gave him along the small of Kip's back.

Oak turns on the radio. "You want hip-hop? Well, you're not going to get it."

"Jazz," Kip says. "88.9."

"You're kidding, right?"

"No." Kip doesn't look at him. "I told you I play piano."

"Jazz piano?"

"Yeah."

If the kid was any weirder, Oak would check him into McLean. Or Harvard.

Oak finds the station. Some saxophone music comes on. There's not a piano in it. But Oak leaves it, he doesn't care. The kid likes it. He doesn't want Kip to feel ashamed about something he's into.

"That's John Coltrane," Kip says.

"I heard of him. You take lessons?"

"From my father."

Oak can't picture the boney guy in his dirty wife-beater in his dead-wife, shit-box house doing much of anything, let alone playing jazz piano.

"My father can play anything. He used to play in Miami.

Puerto Rican jazz. You should see his record collection. It takes up our whole front room. Up the walls. Everywhere."

"Why you guys in Quincy anyway?"

"He wants me to get an education." Kip carefully tapes the molding. "The thing with Coltrane, man, is the sound he gets. No one knows how he did it."

Joan comes into the kitchen holding an empty coffee mug. She looks into the room. "I tried to do it myself." The plum colored slash is still visible beneath the primer. They look at her. It's like a whole conversation goes by. She looks out to the backyard. There's a dead tree half toppled in whatever storm took out the arbor. "I thought I could do it."

The saxophone is wailing now in some kind of jazz freak out. Oak turns it down. Joan stands there, like she's on meds but alert too, just alert to another place.

"We'll take a break," Oak says. Kip comes down from the ladder.

"You want something to drink?" Joan says.

"You got a bathroom?" Oak asks.

"It's down that hall," she says.

Oak nods, takes his boots off. He's wearing skate socks he found in his dresser drawer. Two pairs to make up for the holes. He heads down the hallway, her floorboards wide, old, and shiny. Behind him, he hears Joan asking Kip about school.

Oak finds the bathroom door and opens it. But it's not the bathroom, it's an office, the husband's office. It's filled with books and more so with strange equipment, scientific equipment, old stuff that looks like it would be in a 1950s science lab, or a sci-fi movie. Clunky gray-green machines, metal boxes with dials, microscopes. And there's a narrow bed, to the side of a desk, wedged in. The sheets on the bed are rumpled. The guy's moved downstairs maybe, not out. A Boston College banner. Photographs. The husband and Joan. Their wedding. Joan figure skating. She's maybe eight. Oak sees her in her eyes and in her neck and in her smile. Three thin-bladed swords on a rack on the wall. On a shelf, a fencing helmet. A fencing physicist. He doesn't even know how you meet such a person. Go to law school, maybe.

Oak's PC classes had a hundred, a hundred-fifty people in them. He liked the classes, history, one course in modern American literature, though he couldn't finish the books in time. They put him into Organizational Behavior for a major, where they put all the athletes, with a grad student giving him notes which were basically the answers to the tests.

He's turning to find the actual bathroom when he sees a shelf full of pills. Bottles of them. MS Contin. Roxanol. Something called Compazine. Dexedrine.

He quickly grabs the Contin. Morphine. He grabs the Dexedrine. Industrial strength. He gets out of the husband's room, quietly closes the door, his heart racing in the hall.

The guy's dead.

The paint-slashed wall.

The way she is. The shoes still by the door.

The hallway buckles. He finds the bathroom. He goes inside and locks the door.

He looks at the Dexy bottle. Charles Linney. The prescription was filled in May. He looks at the Oxy bottle. May. They're both nearly full.

Oak gets the top off of the Dexy. Chews two. Gets his head to the tap and washes the bitter powder down. He grabs some toilet paper, shoves it in the bottles so the pills won't rattle when he walks. He hopes she won't notice them missing.

BACK IN THE KITCHEN, Kip's waving his skinny arms around talking. Joan's smiling, but she's looking past Kip too. Kip doesn't see it. Oak watches her from across the dining room, waiting on the Dexy to drop, noticing now the burned-down candles in the silver chandelier, the dining room chairs she would have had to move, the dining room table she had to cover. Joan turns and sees him. A tunnel, their eyes, he feels it, she must.

"You want something to drink?" she says. She's miles gone. Oak hears his heart up in his head. He moves toward her and takes the cup, her eyes uncertain, he sees the photos behind her on the fridge.

"I thought maybe you fell in," Kip says, refilling orange juice from a bottle.

"We'll finish up," Oak says as steady as he can. He thinks again of their shoes side-by-side by the front door. He sees his ma's blue bathrobe hanging on her closet hook.

"I was telling her about Miles Davis," Kip says. "Piano. Trumpet. That dude did it all."

"The primer's gotta dry," Oak says. "I can come back tomorrow."

"I'm not around tomorrow," she says. Maybe she heard him in her husband's office. Maybe she can see something funny in his red eyes.

"You said it was dry out, should only take a couple hours, right?" Kip says.

Oak looks at her. She's looking back again at the air between them where she lives. Oak wants to get out.

"We'll get lunch," he says, "come back in a couple hours maybe."

21

"You don't have to stick around," Oak tells Kip as they get in Arlene's car. "I'll take you home."

"No," Kips says, fast.

Oak looks at him. "I'll just drop you home." He's watching his own hands open and close on the steering wheel. He needs to do something physical, even as doing something physical may lay him out on his back.

"I can use the loot," Kips says quietly.

Kip's looking at him. Oak sees him up that ladder with his beaten back. He sees Joan standing like air in the dining room doorway. Oak doesn't want to go to his mother's house. He doesn't want to go to Arlene's.

"Ah, fuck it," Oak says, the Dexy rising in him. He turns the radio on to Kip's jazz station. He finds a Home Depot on his phone. "We'll fix her arbor."

They drive up Route 9. Kip is talking but Oak's not really hearing much, Kip goes on about jazz guys and how he wishes he had a real piano like the one he saw in Joan's front room. They park in the Brookline Home Depot lot, Kip talking now about grapes.

"Rest it for a while," Oak says, Kip's chatter bouncing around in him, the Contin doing nothing for the dark throb in his bones. But he won't take another. He needs to save it. He needs to skate.

Inside, Kip goes up an aisle by himself. Oak finds the lumber section. He guesses at the right wood for the crossbeams and the posts. He loads the wood onto a pallet. Stands there, looking at the wood, the big overhead fluorescents buzzing and wavering. He goes up the tool aisle, finds Kip looking at a wall of hammers.

"You need something?" Oaks says.

Kip doesn't look up.

"I'm buying. What do you want?"

"A hammer," Kip says. "A nice hammer. Like this one." Kip picks up a gold hammer with a blood-red grip. Oak watches Kip weigh its power. Kip hammers at the air. "I got projects all around my house. But I don't have a good hammer."

Oak knows it's going to be expensive. "Okay. We can put that hammer to use. And we need nails. Tacks."

"She gonna pay us?"

"I'll pay you."

"You rich?"

"Yes."

Kip smiles.

They get to the checkout line. A hundred and four bucks. Kip looks at the total on the register display. "You don't have to buy the hammer."

"I got it," Oak says. He puts down his credit card and waits to see if it will go through.

THEY SIT IN JOAN'S DRIVEWAY with the McDonald's Oak got them. Her car's gone. Oak's zoning, the Dexy firing now in his blood and up in the front part of his brain.

"Call your father and let him know where you are," Oak says.

"I'm all right."

"Call him," Oak says. He doesn't need the dude knocking on his door as well. "And see if she has a shovel or something in her garage."

Oak hands him his phone. Kip gets out of the car, stands in the driveway talking on the phone.

Oak takes the Dexy bottle from his pocket. The cap jumps from his hand and some pills scatter to his lap. Oak chews two more. He'll be flying, but the thought of going back to paint that room spooks him. Like the season he lived in a room inside the rink in Florida. When he walked out of the windowless room, there was the blackened arena, with the shadowy, empty seats, a low black hum rising from the ice. The wavy heat of Florida outside. Black in the room, black outside the door. He couldn't be sure where he was.

Kip brings a shovel from her garage. Oak hustles the pills back into the bottle, gets the toilet paper back in, fumbles with the cap. When he shoves the bottle back into his pants, he sees Kip watching him.

"Come on." Oak gets out of the car, walks over to her broken arbor. He hauls it upright. It's just a store-bought arbor, he sees that now, cheap, lightweight, and tangled in vines. A lot of glue and staples. He probably could have bought a new one at Home Depot for less than he paid for the wood. "Dig that shovel in there."

Kip digs. Oak jams a post in. Kip pounds the dirt.

"Okay, and that one."

They work the second post.

"Good," Oak says.

Oak hauls up the lattice and vines. When he does it, he feels the scar tissue on his hand open and his knuckles bleed.

"I can do the hammering," Kip says. Kip's holding his new gold hammer and the box of nails.

"Okay, tap one in there, and there." They work the other side. "You're a natural," Oak says, and Kip seems to concentrate even more after Oak says it, a serious look on the kid's face. Kip pounds the last strip, the arbor lopsided but standing.

"You ready to launch?" Oak says.

Kip nods.

Oak steps back. Kip jumps out from under the vines, shaking dead leaves from his hair.

The thing holds.

"Now that's an arbor!" Kip says grinning.

Oak laughs. The air's vibrating. It sounds good to hear Kip clapping and laughing.

"We're gonna get drunk in the spring on grapes!" Kip says.

Joan's car pulls into the driveway.

"We fixed your arbor," Kip says when Joan comes over holding a bag of groceries.

She looks at Oak. "You all right?"

Oak wipes his face with his sleeve, sees the sweat and blood. "The thing was rotted out on two sides."

She nods.

"I'm not going to charge you or anything," Oak says.

"Now you can have wine," Kip says. "Or grape jelly."

Joan smiles. "It looks good."

"It's a surprise," Kip says.

Joan looks at Oak, shakes her head. Oak goes to her car to see if there's another bag of groceries to carry in. There's one more bag. He carries it after her into the house. He sets the groceries on the humming kitchen table. He glances down the wavering hallway to her dead husband's office.

"How do you know him?" Joan says, putting groceries into the refrigerator.

He turns from the hall. "We go way back to when he got the shit knocked out of him by a bunch of his pals."

When he turns, the kitchen lifts and he bounces against the table.

"Tim—"

He has to lean against the kitchen wall. He gets his breath. He closes his eyes tightly and feels an icy sweat pop from his pores. "We'll come back. Next Sunday. To finish up."

"What's going on?"

"It's just my head. Those cops," he partially lies. "I'm good." He gets out of the house and down the front steps. Kip is waiting in the yard, looking up at the sky.

"You see a lot of sky here," Kip says, watching a plane. "And it's quiet."

"That sky costs a lot of money," Oak says. He puts an arm on the kid to steady himself. "And so does that quiet." Oak nods at Joan who's standing in the doorway, watching. Kip waves to her when he realizes they won't be going back inside.

DRIVING, OAK COULD THREAD ARLENE'S VOYAGER sideways through two lines of trucks if he had to. He's watching the speedometer, he's forcing himself to stop for a three count at the stop signs.

Kip's asleep. As soon as they got in the car, as soon as Kip knew he was going home, Kip had his head against the doorframe and was sleeping. Oak sees again how young he is. Skinny. Kip's got primer on his cheek, a dead leaf in his hair. When they get to Quincy Center, Kip suddenly wakes up and says, "You can let me out here."

"I'll take you home."

"I'm meeting someone."

Oak looks at him. Kip rubs his eyes. Puffs up his hair.

"Here is fine. At the Dunkin' Donuts."

Oak drops him off. He watches Kip go inside, his new hammer in his hand. He watches Kip orders two doughnuts and a drink. Kip brings them to a table, sets the hammer down. He sits alone eating the doughnuts. Maybe he is waiting on a friend, Oak thinks. Or maybe he just wanted doughnuts.

OAK DRIVES HARD ALONG THE OCEAN, to see it, for no reason, Sea Street to Houghs Neck. Rock Island Cove. Gets fast onto 3A, pushing the Voyager. The shore houses speed by. The car windows open, he's soaking with sweat. Boats, dry-docked and wrapped for winter. He burns up Nantasket Avenue, guns it through as a light turns red, smooth, he's feeling light, some kind of xylophone solo on the radio, the sun falling behind him, dropping over Boston, orange against the cold, gray water, the blue in with the gray, the purple. Irish flags. Statues bending outside Our Savior by the Sea. Statues bending outside the homes beneath the Irish flags. Seagulls. Dolphin mailboxes. You had cactus ones in El Paso. *Some prick must live there, ha-ha.* Keeping up with the xylophone, smacking the dash as the Voyager flies through Hull, the Christmas lights blurring. To the tip, to the stony beach. Oak pulls over, his eyes strobing.

Oak stares for a minute out the windshield at the choppy water, the waves crashing, his own wave crashing. Squantum. The Harbor Islands. Joan's dead husband. He didn't kill him. He steps out into the cold air. He sits on the beach rocks. Beyond them, Harbor Island, the Sugar Bowl, Carson Beach.

He's always liked the Southie ocean. To look out, after a run, at dawn, to see the sun coming up, it gave him a kind of hope, the wave tops, the gulls. Ireland if you kept going. Europe. In west Texas, the desert goes on like an ocean. It looked like there was nothing there, but then he walked it, and the more he walked it, the more he found: cactus in all shapes, birds, lizards. Prairie dogs popped their heads out. Mesquite and mule deer and beetles. And in Michigan, he liked the cold, green hills. The soft Carolina water outside Wilmington that was like bathwater. His first summer in North Carolina, he and six guys lived in a house on the Wilmington River, not far from the beach, building condos with the Mexicans. He'd skate with the kids at the local rink. The little kids were the best, stutter-stepping, grabbing their parents' hand, bear-hugging his legs. Some of them had little skate-walkers, they were like ninety-year-olds inching along the ice. Oak was twenty-four then, and they'd form a chain off each of his hands, boys and girls, and he would spin them and then snap them away, the kids screaming, happy, some landing on their asses, the older ones asking him to watch them skate, to sign their T-shirts and hats.

Oak gets his boots off. Rolls up his sweats. He walks into the icy water. Feels rocks beneath his feet. He looks across the bay, the sweat on his forehead like Vaseline. His ma humming now, under the ground. Joan alone at her kitchen table. Alone at the bar. Kip with vines in his hair. McDonald's face broken on the ice. Humming. He could have taught Kate to skate. He could have taken her to Murphy's Rink or to the skating pond in the Common, to skate under the holiday lights.

22

Stick-slap against the ice, the hard slap at face-off, snapping graphite, and Oak sees two boys reflected in the board glass, and then there's knocking. Oak slams a guy's head to the glass, a whole party of kids flashing their phones, it rushes on him, his mouth is paper dry, his skin is wet and cold, his eyes are stuck together, and suddenly he sees Tommy and Jack, his nephews, Arlene's kids, their hands against a car window, knocking. Oak finds himself in the Voyager driver's seat, the Voyager angled, he sees it now, across Arlene's front lawn.

He doesn't know how he got there.

He sits up. He holds a monster rush down, shivering in thick sweat, the Voyager windows are laced with snow. He smiles at his nephews, eases the window down. The sun's not fully up.

"You all right, Uncle Tim?"

"You all right, Uncle Oak?"

"I must have fallen asleep."

"I saw you from the bathroom window."

"We saw you."

"Did you wake your mother?"

"No."

"Good."

He'll hoof it to the bus stop. Wait on the T to open.

23

Oak gets Slats on the phone.

"We were set up," Slats says. "Ivan was. Only and the Georgians called the cops. Some kind of bitch-slap statement, if you can believe it."

Oak can believe it. It's like Slats to get punked by Georgians. In Dorchester, Massachusetts.

"One of the Mexicans fell off the roof," Slats says.

Oak feels his stomach again. "What Mexican?"

"The fat one."

"Esteban. How is he?"

"How the fuck should I know? Are you even listening, Oak? It was a set-up. We're lucky we got away."

"I want to see Kate." He just says it.

"Zink says Only says not to worry. Everything's taken care of. We're not going to see our money though . . ."

"Kevin. Did you hear what I said?"

Out the window, sunlight's coming up the road.

"Chickie Mulligan died, did you hear that, Oak? He went to

hairdressing school. Had a heart attack. And Carol Gardner. She had triplets. No one knows for sure who the father is. Could be three men's the joke . . . And speaking of fathers, mine's still dead, but my mother's alive, thanks for asking. And no disrespect. She's still in the Bricks, still growing her window plants. And my sisters are good."

"Slats—"

"Because I haven't seen you, Oak. Not holidays. Not Christmas. Birthdays. The years pile on."

"I get it."

"I'm getting gray hairs around my dick."

"I fucking get it, Kevin. Kate's my daughter."

For a minute there's nothing on the other end.

"No one's stopping you, Tim. I told you that in the diner. Talk to Shannon."

A text comes in from Barry.

You on your way?

"Oak, you there?" Slats says.

"Yeah. I gotta go, Kevin. I gotta go work out."

24

Old Colony, the Bricks, is being leveled for new welfare town houses. There are signs up. HUD. New public houses, but no new jobs except for the out-of-town builders. A half-mile away, on the Point, houses sell for over a million.

Oak stands on the ball field across the street. He's got a duffel bag of Uncle Barry's weed. A pound wrapped in gym clothes that smell like Barry's dog. Slats lived in OC when they were kids. Slats's place was nice, his mother had plants all over it. Old Colony was okay once you got out of the hallways.

Oak stands there on the ice-hard grass. Holding a bag. Like a criminal. Barry said to use the baseball diamond because there's no cameras on the ballfield. He's standing there in the sharp November daylight, with a duffel of chickenshit black market weed, so he can skate. Across the outfield grass, two black teenaged girls roll toward him on their bikes. The bike tires crunch the frozen grass.

"Friend of Lauren's?" the younger one, maybe she's fourteen, says.

Oak nods. The other girl takes the bag from him and they are riding away before he even has a chance to say anything. Two girls with a gym bag, two black girls riding back to school, riding the weed to someone older who will tell them what to do.

25

Oak goes to the Portuguese bakery and gets some cookies that look like Mexican buñuelos. In case they're no good, he goes to Dunkin' Donuts and buys a dozen doughnuts. He doesn't know what Esteban's going to do with a dozen cookies plus a dozen doughnuts, but he's hoping the guy's got more visitors than just him.

The girl at the hospital desk looks at him like he's a patient. She finds Esteban's name, gives Oak the room number. Makes Oak sign in, show his ID. "Texas," she says.

Oak finds Esteban's room. Esteban's in there with two other patients in the triple room, each looking bad but not as bad as Esteban whose head is in a metal crown. But he grins big when he sees Oak.

"Oak! Jefe!"

They eat a couple doughnuts each. Esteban tells him that his actual name is Emilio Lopez, that he's fucked now—once his neck and back is healed they'll ship him back to Chihuahua. Esteban bites into a cream-filled doughnut. The way his head's angled, he sugars himself. Oak brushes it off him.

"My mother she used to make buñuelos. They were terrible!" Esteban says. "But my grandmother, she used to make a three-milk cake. That was like heaven. And nopales. She could cook. You go to the hospital and all you can think about is food!"

A guy from another bed says something Oak can't understand, deep in a drug dream. It's spooky, the place is like a death room.

"The thing with three-milk cake, Oak, is you have to do it slow. No one does slow no more. My wife, she's rush, rush, rush. And my oldest daughter? She wants a new phone, she wants a motor scooter." Esteban smiles. "They all want things, Oak, when things cost money."

"We were set up."

"I know. Of course."

Oak nods.

"They don't know how it's going to heal. My back. There's a Panamanian doctor. 'Maybe,' he says. But they never say no, Panamanians."

Oak doesn't know what to say. "You'll be okay."

"Thank you, Oak. For coming to see me in this place. I'm sorry I have nothing to give you. Wait. Here, here—"

Esteban reaches around the nightstand.

"They cut my chain off. It's here. Take it—"

A gold cross on a broken chain.

"Nah—"

"*Si, si*, take it—"

"No. It's yours, for you. Thank you, though. Thank you."

Esteban nods.

"I'll come back and see you again."

Esteban takes his hand.

26

Shark's on his way out when Oak gets in. "You ain't fit for a janitor," Shark says.

"That's why I'm here."

"Your blood's not right. You look puffy."

"I'll get there."

Shark buttons his coat.

"You just going home?" Oak asks.

"Slept some on the sofa." Shark grabs some towels that are in a pile by the free mats, carries them to the hamper that hangs by the mirror behind the heavy bags. "You're delusional, Oak. I want you to get to a doctor, see what's going on."

"Hey—" He's pissed. Shark's old, Oak's not. Even with his body the way it is, he could launch Jim Sharkey across the office and into the wall.

Shark looks at him coolly, standing by the black hanging bags. "You got something to say, Tim?"

He doesn't.

"Buckets are by the bathroom." Shark walks past Oak, past his ring, toward his metal front door. "And do my office, too."

OAK EMPTIES THE BUCKETS into the bathroom sink. The toilet is backed up and filled with shit. He knows Shark knows, there's no way Shark missed this. It's not the shit, he doesn't care, there's a plunger and a brush, it's that Shark does this to him, feels like he has to test him, again, he almost says fuck it and leaves it for Shark to find in the morning. But he cleans it.

Choices, Shark would yell. Oak studied the handout Shark made, a chart of all the best places on the body to land a punch. *Choices*: Oak knocking a Charlestown kid over the ropes and didn't the Irish parents love that. *Choices*: Shannon and him warm in a blanket at the fort by the water, feeling smart and grown. *Choices*: the duffel bag of weed for the teenage girls at Old Colony, the drugs in his own system. His father would be asleep downstairs in the living room chair, waking to drive Oak to the ring or the rink, stopping for egg sandwiches and coffee.

His father bolted. One day he was under the trains with Shark, taking Oak to 6:00 a.m. and midnight skates, and then he was gone. He drank and then he ran. He just took off. Oak remembers his parents' fights, his father driving off in his car. Coming home drunk, later, half the time with flowers. Flowers that half the time his mother threw in the garbage or out onto the front steps and half the time she put in a vase on the kitchen table.

His father left when Oak was a freshman at PC. When Kate was born. His father never saw her. His father was living on the Cape and he called Oak and Arlene, drunk, saying he just felt that he was suffocating in his life and that he didn't expect them to understand.

His ma called her husband that first summer to tell him about his granddaughter. "He won't visit," his ma said to Oak when she got off the phone, "He says he will, but he won't." He didn't.

He came down to PC once in Oak's sophomore year, and he and Oak had dinner and Oak showed him photos of Kate on his phone. She was one. Shannon was coming down some weekends when the team was in Providence. And then Shannon was coming down less and less and Oak was never going up there. His ma was dating and for a while she was running out of control. His mother and sister were at his college graduation. By then, he and Shannon were barely seeing each other and Kate was two. His father had moved to New Hampshire. His father took up the Bible and had a girlfriend and he wrote Oak a long email apologizing for running and offered to send him some money from his new job working maintenance on Peter Pan buses. His father asked, again, about his granddaughter and said he hoped to visit soon. Oak just told him he was moving to Michigan, he didn't even tell him about the AHL, and that he didn't hold it against him that he'd split.

He didn't. He was out of the house. Arlene was out of the house. If his old man didn't want to stay with his wife, Oak wasn't going to tell him that he should. His father was barely home. His ma was barely home. His father was out with his friends, she was out with hers. They didn't dance any longer, they didn't talk. They barely found time to watch TV together.

And then in Florida, a couple years back, his father emailed again. Oak barely checked his email—his was still his Providence College address. He'd gone into the account to try to remember the name of a guy who worked in the team office whose uncle worked with the Flyers. He remembered his password because he just used his name. He was five years out of Grand Rapids when his father asked in the email how Michigan was going. Oak figured the five years passed were an indication of how his father was going, with no word from him, no money sent to Oak's ma he guessed, and a move to Florida. They had that in common, a Florida collapse. Again, his old man told him about Jesus. And about how he wanted to see him. He didn't mention his granddaughter. His old man was maybe a two-hour drive away. Oak didn't respond.

HE GETS THE BATHROOM DONE, goes out to the gym floor. He'll clean the mats and the bags after he dirties them. He gets a jump rope. He ate one of the dead husband's Dexy. When he's done, he'll do an Oxy 30. He's got twenty-five days before Worcester.

His heart feels right. It beats steady as he swings the rope, and he's landing okay, with small, quick hops, the ankle, the knee, the hip, holding. He picks up the pace. The rope snaps the floor, whirs the air, bubbling him. The sweat feels good. He drop squats. Everything holds. Does twenty. He gets on the floor. Knocks out twenty jump-backs. His hip and back and shoulder are okay. At the heavy bag, when his hands split and blood creeps over his fingers and palms, he works the bag harder, to beat himself a tougher skin.

27

Arlene's at the house at lunchtime when he gets back from buying eggs. She's pissed. She's got a box of their ma's Christmas stuff on the kitchen table. She's drinking white wine.

"You think I wouldn't know, Tim? You think they wouldn't tell me? My car was parked halfway on the lawn."

She's got the Christmas decorations spread out on the table, sorting.

"I'm not used to lawns, Arlene."

"Go fuck yourself, Timmy."

She's packing the decorations she wants into a plastic crate.

"They want to look up to you, Tim. Uncle Oak."

"Save it, Arlene."

His sister lights a cigarette. "You want one?"

"Yeah." He smokes it for her, to apologize.

"You look like shit," she says.

"So do you. What's going on?"

"Kyle and I are fighting."

"He fights?"

"You're an asshole."

"I know. I'm sorry."

"You need a doctor. Is your team paying for . . . any of this?"

He sits next to his sister at the kitchen table. He picks up a wooden advent calendar, spins the days. "I got jumped by two cops."

"They arrest you?"

He nods.

"What's happened, Tim? What's happening?"

"I'm all right."

"Kyle will know a lawyer."

"I'm all right."

"She left the house to both of us," Arlene says, nodding at a yellow real estate folder she brought over. "It's almost paid for. And Kyle's doing all right. You can just live here."

"That's your money, Arlene. For you and your kids."

"We never see Kate." She wraps a donkey and a star. "You can't read your own obituary, Tim."

He starts to tell her to go fuck herself, checks himself, stands. He puts the advent calendar in the crate.

"You left the burner on, Tim. I came in and it was glowing red."

He leaves his sister in the kitchen with the boxes of ornaments, the stove, the real estate folder, and the half-drunk bottle of wine.

THE WIND BLOWS COLD OFF THE BAY. Barry's walking his dog in the morning sun out along the Fort. His uncle's got a cap on. Barry looks like Oak's grandfather and the years since Oak was young are there for him in a flash.

"This is a good way to pick up girls, Timmy. Get yourself a little companion. Get one with teeth like Niamh here, keeps the husbands away as well."

Barry lets the dog go. Niamh drags its leash toward the water. His Uncle pulls out a smoke, offers one to Oak.

"I'm good."

"So how's the come-back?"

"Good."

"Good to hear. Good. We was always proud of you, Timmy. In the ring. On the ice." Barry cups a light. Exhales. Tosses the match to the grass. "And getting an education. That matters."

He's not sure if his uncle is fucking with him. He can't tell if Barry is being sarcastic. His uncle must know why they're meeting. They're not sat in a snug for beer and conversation.

His uncle looks across the bay, into the sunlight and wind. Barry's blue eyes catch the sky. He sees Barry on the boat Barry had. Sees him lying knife-slashed behind the school.

"I think, Tim," his uncle says into the wind, "if I had done a better education. If the schools weren't so fucked up. Ah well, that's pissing in the wind. There weren't any jobs anyway when I was your age. Drive a cement truck. Move to Quincy and work in some shit office."

Barry blows a line of smoke. "Everything good at the ballfield?"

Oak nods.

"Good."

"I need something for right now, Barry. Something to get me through December. To get me through like I was."

"Like you were?"

"Strong."

"Boston strong," Barry says. "The mighty Oak. Yeah." Barry

inhales, looks out at the water. Exhales. "You try what I gave you?"

Barry means the heroin. "No."

"Can you sell it?"

His uncle's looking at him now.

"I'm not saying it's a good thing, Tim. But supply and demand, you know? I lead my life. I'm not telling others how to lead theirs."

"Yeah." Oak says it fast.

"Yeah as in yes, you can sell it?"

Oak nods and that's the only thing he feels, his neck and his chin nodding. The rest of him feels stone cold and he knows in that cold inside that he is taking a step toward killing himself. "For a little while."

Barry puts a hand on his shoulder. "Start small, a delivery, sort of to a hub like. See how it goes, nephew."

Niamh comes up, a crushed can in her mouth. The dog drops the can at Oak's feet. Uncle Barry hands Oak an envelope of pills.

"You've made a friend," Barry says, bending down to rub the dog behind the ears.

28

Oak's mother's car is up at the far end of the driveway, near their small back area. A hunter green Pontiac sedan with a dent and a side scrape. He gets into the front seat, slides the seat back, and jams the keys into the ignition. It starts. There's a pack of smokes stuck in the visor. There are CDs because the car has a CD player: Rod Stewart's Christmas album, Cher, Leo Sayer. Oak opens the glove compartment. Maps. Receipts. Her registration. Some pens. He's looking for blow, he's not fooling himself, she kept it around sometimes he knew. The car smells like her. He's probably imagining it, but it does. He backs out of the driveway, swings the Bonneville into drive.

Oak finds a decent-looking Christmas wreath at the 7-11. He drives to Joan's house. He's jumping around so much inside that he puts the Leo Sayer on. If he calls her, she'll say no. He wants to see her. He knows that a wreath on the door might only remind her of what she's lost, but it will be going forward, too, that's what he wants her to know, that you have to keep moving.

He pulls into Joan's driveway. There's another car parked there. He walks up her walkway underneath the arbor with the wreath. He sees Kip with his new gold hammer, telling her she'll have grapes in the summer. He sees her standing lost in her kitchen doorway. He sees her dead husband's room. He knocks.

Joan answers. She's in a black turtleneck and jeans. Shoes with heels. "Tim?" She sounds like maybe she's been drinking.

"I got you a wreath. For your door."

"What are you doing here?"

He sees his breath in front of him.

"Wreath?" A guy comes out of the living room, holding a beer, and Oak can smell the paint and then there's another woman there as well. She's holding a glass of wine.

They're looking at him. Not hard, not like he doesn't belong, but curious, like he doesn't belong there now.

"Who's this, Joan?" the woman says.

"This is Tim," Joan says.

He nods at them. He waits for her to say "my client," but she doesn't. She's watching him.

"I'm Ann, Joan's sister," the woman says. "And this is my husband, James."

"We're going bowling," Joan says, steady.

"And we're running late," the sister says. The sister is staring at him now and he doesn't like it. He stares back at her.

"You should come." The husband says it and he is drunk. "Joan? Right? Ann?"

"James," the sister says, and Oak sees her quickly shake her head.

For a minute, no one says anything.

"I just came to drop this off."

Joan is staring at her sister. She doesn't look at him. "Yes. Join us, Tim," Joan says, and she leaves the foyer fast and he's standing there with the sister and the husband and the wreath.

"The more the merrier," the husband says. He sucks back the beer.

"I went to Newton North," Oak says, lying about the local high school for rich kids, to say something.

THEY GO TO A HIPSTER BOWLING BAR in Jamaica Plain. Oak followed them in his ma's car. He sees what's happening. The sister is trying to get Joan to go out. It makes sense. The bar is down a flight of stairs. They've got a dozen lanes on one side, a bar in the middle strung with colored lights, and a small bandstand with some guys playing shoegazer music off to the side.

The husband watches Oak struggle out of his shoes. "You all right, buddy?" the husband says.

"Car wreck."

"Jesus," the guy says. The husband got drinks, Harpoon beer in plastic cups. They asked Oak what he does. He told them he was in real estate.

Joan is standing at the small table, holding the bowling shoes her sister got her.

"Joan can really bowl," the sister says. "Our parents used to take us all the time. Bowling and ping pong."

The husband types names into the electronic score sheet.

Oak sips his beer. Joan just stands there. Around them, people are laughing, there is the rumble of the lanes, the music from the band, the bursting of pins.

"I have to use the bathroom," Joan says. "I'll be right back." Her voice is sharp. It jumps right through him. He stands.

The sister watches her go. He's standing there.

The husband takes his wife's hand. "You know about Charles," the husband says to Oak.

"Who are you, anyway?" the sister says, almost at the same time.

"She's not herself," the husband says.

"She's exactly herself," the sister says, picking up her beer.

Oak sees Joan push through the thick black curtains at the foot of the stairs.

He goes after her. He pushes through the curtains and climbs the stairs to the street. He doesn't see her and then he does. She's leaning on an iron churchyard fence, staring up to the rooftops in a flurry of snow.

"Joan."

"I couldn't stand there."

She gets out a pack of smokes. Her hands shake so badly that he has to take one from the pack for her. He holds it out for her and she takes it from him with her lips. She finds a lighter in her pocket, lights it, inhales, blows smoke up into the flurry and the spotlights of the church.

"Like a double date . . ." she says into the light.

"I don't know what I'm doing here."

She looks at him.

She blows out a long breath and then she seems suddenly calm. "The Assistant DA is pushing for a trial date, Tim. He's bluffing."

"I saw you."

"What?"

"Before. You were sitting in Donahue's, drinking coffee."

She nods. She looks at him. "I go there sometimes. Before

this public defender work. Drink coffee. I saw you there, too," she says. "And then I heard about the incident. A fucked up local hockey star. I asked for your case."

"You're going to save me."

Her eyes tear. When her tears roll down her cheeks he has his arm around her against the cold. He doesn't know why he said it.

"I don't save, Tim."

"Me neither. I'm sorry. I'm really fucking sorry." He's trying to block the wind with his body. "I saw your husband's room."

"Oh. Yeah. This whole thing, Tim, the last year and a half, it's a long, sad dream."

Her face is close. "It's freezing," he says, gently. "I'm freezing. Come on," he says.

He leads them back to the warmth of the club at least so she can get her jacket and go.

They stand inside the heavy curtain. There's an empty table in the back corner near the small stage where three skinny kids in cowboy hats are swapping out gear.

"Let's sit over there. For a minute," he says.

She nods. "I'll just use the bathroom."

He sees her sister and husband watching from across the room. They don't come over. He goes to the bar and orders two Jacks and takes them to the empty table by the stage.

When Joan comes back, he can see she's been crying, that she's put water on her face. She sits beside him, the light of a votive candle across her.

She's sort of shaking her head, talking in there, spinning the candle in her hands.

"Kip thought you should have a wreath," he says, to say something.

She shakes her head, smiles. "And you thought you'd deliver it."

"I wanted to steal his thunder."

She smiles again. But she is dreamy, leaning in and out of the candlelight. "You told them you were in real estate?" she says.

"It's a hockey joke." He drinks the Jack in a swallow.

She looks at her glass, like she's only just seen it. She sips the drink. "I'll talk with the assistant DA," she says, the Jack floating there in her hand like she's forgotten it already.

"I don't want to talk about my case."

She nods. "My sister never even liked Charles . . . It's such bullshit." Joan shakes her head. "I know they're trying to help." She looks at Oak suddenly. "Your mother died."

"Yeah."

"It's different," she says.

"Of course it is." The band starts to play a Willie Nelson song he likes. Oak stands. "Come on." He puts his hand out. He sees it there suspended in the air between them. Joan takes it. Her hand is cold. He wants to stick it in his guts, to warm her.

The dance floor is five tables shoved out of the way. Oak gets a hand to the small of her back. She's tall, but still his hand feels like a mitt on her body. They move together.

"You can dance," Joan says.

"My old man."

The band slows and segues, there's a woman with a fiddle, and it goes quiet when she plays. Joan closes her eyes. He feels the space between them, warm like before.

"This okay?" he says.

Joan doesn't say anything.

He closes his eyes, too, and he finds her, in the quiet behind the music. Joan leans closer. She brings her cheek to the place between his shoulder and his chest. He can smell the soft smell of her hair and the warm smell of her skin. He holds her.

When the song ends, she looks at her hand pressed in his. Keeps looking at it. He sees the knots and the scars and the bruises. She nods, slightly, and draws her hand away.

"I should go back," she says.

When she turns from him, she stumbles a little. He catches her arm. "I'm okay," she says, but suddenly she looks uncertain and her face has gone red at the edges with sweat. She pushes from him.

29

He wakes on a mat on the floor of Shark's gym. The blue mat confuses him and for a flash he thinks it's the blue line and he is for some reason laying on the ice. Oak gets to his feet. Checks his phone. It's 4:00 a.m.

Oak gets back on the stationary bike. He tightens the crank until he has to stand to pedal it. He has sixteen days until the Worcester tryout. Sixteen days to be able to not just last but to dominate. Rob Kellet said he knows what he can do. Oak's getting his head straight. He's getting his body right. The cops, the Albuquerque sissy punches, his back and shoulder surgeries, and his barking hip are just setbacks. He's moving forward. The pills help his head. They help his body. He gets off the bike. He does a hundred mountain climbers and everything holds. On the twenty-fifth burpee, though, his hip gives and Oak falls sideways to the mat. He slaps it. He puts his body in a bird-dog plank. Holds it. His spine starts burning. He holds it some more, he is in charge. He sees Joan's face in candlelight, he sees her looking up into the snow. He feels her close to him, dancing. She'll be home now, probably not sleeping, thinking about her dead husband. He lowers to his knees.

His arms and both shoulders feel good. He's been pounding water and creatine and whey. Eggs and instant oatmeal. He gets up from the mat to take a piss. In Shark's bathroom mirror, he looks into his own eyes. Same guy staring back. His face is banged up, his beard needs work, but he doesn't look like a guy who's done. He's got two weeks. He chews an Oxy so he can get home and into his mother's armchair to rest his body. His head won't rest. He's given up on that. He tries to focus it across the hurting nights on the ice. On corner plays. Goal-face chop-ups. Grinding. Joan's husband wasn't going to use the pills. He sees the girls on the Old Colony baseball diamond with the weed. Barry with the gun in his drawer. And for a minute he worries. But he's getting strong again, stronger than Derek Boogaard, the New York Ranger winger who was found dead beside a coffee can of pills; stronger than Rick Rypien of the Vancouver Canucks who was found hanging dead from a beam in his basement; stronger than Wade Belak of the Leafs, Panthers, and Predators who was found hanging from a shower rod. Bob Probert dead on his powerboat with his burst heart and brain. Junior Seau with a shotgun to his head. Todd Ewan of the Mighty Ducks with a gunshot to the head. Steve Montador. Their piles of money untouched in their banks. Their children left alone. He read that Belak had a hundred fights. That Boogaard had twenty concussions from blows to the head. Oak can't count the minutes disappeared on the scoreboard clock. Sometimes whole periods went by before he came to. Boogaard was twenty-eight. Rypien, twenty-seven. Belak, thirty-five. Probert was forty-five. When Probert's family shipped his brain to Boston University, they found it was rotten with CTE.

Oak shakes it off. They don't even fight in the NHL any-more—the No Hit League. And where would Gretzky have been without Semenko and McSorly? Like Sidney Crosby, lying in the hospital maybe. Oak doesn't know. He flushes the toilet. He's not pissing blood. The doctor was wrong about that. He knows about CTE. He knows that he forgets stuff. And it's not the big hits, it's the little ones, and if he starts worrying about all the little hits he's taken since he was five—the shoulders to the chin, the uppercuts and jabs, the board crashes—he may as well lie down in his boy-hood bed and die. When he's dead, he'll worry about CTE.

Oak turns back to the mirror over the sink. He nods at the beast nodding back. He first heard that Willie Nelson song, "Sis-ter's Coming Home," in Texas. Joan wasn't going to save him. He doesn't require saving. He's not going to save her. He wouldn't know how. He watches himself as he turns for the door and disappears.

John the teacher and his kid are there, and two firefighters are coming in, a man and a woman. It's 5:00 a.m.

John comes over, smiling, holding a coffee. "You working here now?"

"Working to work out, yeah."

John looks over at his son JJ, who's hitting the heavy bag. "JJ was pretty excited to meet you the other day."

JJ spins a stupid back fist.

"Let me ask you something, Oak, if you don't mind." John watches his son deliver a roundhouse to the bag, the kid slipping backward from his own kick. "What do you think of the whole MMA business?"

"It's not boxing."

"That's for sure."

John drinks some coffee. "St. Cath's skates at Murphy's Rink every Wednesday. It'd be great if you could come by. The kids would love it. I know JJ would get a big kick out of it. I sort of help out. The ice is still shit by the way."

Oak looks at him, at his soft, grinning face.

"I got to do the bathroom floor."

30

On Thanksgiving Day Oak rides the T out to his sister's in Stoneham. They used to go to the Stoneham Zoo on school trips, see the elephants. He's got two grocery bags filled with Yukon Golds, green cabbage, and leeks. Kyle's at the T-station, with the boys in his car, both kids in Holy Cross hoodies.

In the car, Oak turns to look at his nephews, who sit there quiet, in the back, not looking at him. "The other night," Oak says. "I'm sorry I scared you."

"You were drunk," the big one, Tommy, says.

"I was."

"I want to apologize to both of you." He thinks hard, to get their names. "Jack. Tommy."

"He was scared," Jack says about his big brother.

"Shut up," Tommy says.

"I was stupid," Oak says.

Kyle nods. "We've all been there."

"No," Oak says. "Your father's better than that."

"Then why did you do it?" Tommy asks.

"I don't know."

ARLENE'S HITTING THE WHITE WINE PRETTY GOOD, but he's not one to say anything. He's drinking Kyle's beer, trying not to drink it all. He learned how to make stump, colcannon, as a kid from his mother's mother. She was a tough lady, and his ma didn't get on with her very well, but Oak liked her. He liked that there was a food called stump. He likes cutting up the vegetables, the sound of the oil in the pan, getting in the right amount of black pepper and salt. Doing the onions so they are soft but not gutted.

He peels the potatoes, chops them, and puts them in the pot. Kyle's floating around, half-watching Thanksgiving football with his sons, who mostly are on their phones.

"Here," Arlene says, and she's got a forkful of stuffing she's dug out of the chest of the roasting turkey.

He blows on it, gets it in his mouth. "It's really good."

"Ma used to use Bells, remember?"

"No."

"You remember how it wasn't that good?"

"It was fine."

"She was a lousy cook." Arlene laughs. "I got that from her."

"Come on, this is beautiful."

"The stuffing is Kyle's mother's recipe." And suddenly his sister's laugh turns into a quick gulp of crying. She turns her face from him.

"Hey—"

"You think about that she's dead?"

"Of course I do."

"And dad, whatever."

Oak nods.

"My own kids. Tommy. He hates me, Tim."

"Come on—"

"He won't talk to me. He doesn't listen to me. He's fucking up in school."

"He's a kid, a boy. He'll come around."

"When do I come around, Tim?"

He carefully sets the fork down.

"I don't have any time, Tim. I never have. First, there was dad's drinking, then ma, alone, smoking, doing blow—"

"She didn't do that much."

"Tim, you were gone."

"I was skating."

"I came home every weekend from Holy Cross. And then Kyle, and now Tommy and Jack."

His sister buries her glass, sucks snot back up her nose. She wipes her face.

"Shannon had Kate, Tim. You had Kate. You have her. I don't know, Kyle and I, we maybe could have had a child who loves me."

At that, he's not happy. She's pushed it too far. He feels suddenly manipulated, like she wants something from him. Like she's blaming him for her life.

"Look, let's just eat dinner, okay, Arlene? That stuffing was really good, and the turkey smells great." Oak carries a basket of bread to the table.

When the meal's half done and they've had wine and the kids are bored, Arlene says, "You can stay in the house, Tim. Get a job coaching. When you get better. You like kids."

"A bouncer while you wait," Kyle says.

"Bouncer," Jack says.

They've talked more about it, he can tell.

"Tommy and Jack would be glad to see more of you."

Oak looks at the kids. At best, they couldn't give a shit.

"St. Anthony's would hire you, right? When you get better."

"I don't see anything wrong with him," Kyle says.

"You better get your eyes fixed," Oak says.

Jack laughs.

Tommy has his phone out in his lap.

"Tommy. Your uncle's here," Arlene says.

The kid doesn't look up. "Don't tell me what to do."

"Hey—" Kyle says, without a lot of game.

"Hey, what?" Tommy says, looking up to glare at Arlene.

"I don't have four hundred and ninety-five thousand dollars, Arlene." Oak stands. "Come on—" he says to the boys who were asking him about hockey in the car, Kyle probably talking him up on the drive to the station. "I'll show you bozos how to roof it."

"There's pie."

"We want to go outside, Mum," Jack says.

Tommy has already left the table.

THEY HAVE A NET IN THE GARAGE, so maybe the kids really are interested. They drag the net into the driveway. Oak closes the garage door. A two-car garage.

"All right," he says. "Think of the net as four boxes. Box one, lower left. Box two, lower right. Box three, upper right. Box four, upper left. When you bring the stick back, you just think about that box. Nothing else. Not the goalie, not the puck. Just say the box out loud in your head, loud, keep your chin in, and smack it. Follow through. Let the stick be a whip. Bang!"

That's what Coughlin told him at St. Ant's when he was twelve. It made a difference. Makes a difference. Like a whip, not solid. Crack the whip at the end. Let the slapper snap.

"Hold on," Tommy gets into the Zdeno jersey that's hanging on the back of the net. Jack's making like he's skating around. "I want a stick," Jack says.

"Yeah, you should have one."

"He's too small."

"No way," Oak says. "He's not too small. We'll find something."

He can't believe his sister, getting one brother a twig and not the other. Oak rummages around the garage. He sees Kyle's golf bag. He gets Kyle's five-iron Ping.

"I'm Zdeno," Tommy's saying. Oak barely follows the NHL anymore. But it's good, that the kid's a fan.

"I'm Oak!" Jack says as Oak hands him his father's five iron, the kid's face lighting up.

He lines them up ten feet from the net. "You start here, you can shoot or come at me. But if you come at me, I'm coming at you."

They've got a puck and a ball. "Let Jack use the ball," Oak says. He gets in the net. Jack winds up and sparks the Ping right into the blacktop. "Keep your head in there," Oak says, grinning. They start knocking shots at him, pretending to skate around, charging the net, Oak blocking a couple to keep them honest, roaring at them, his nephews scared and laughing, letting most go by, for them and for him.

"Box three! Box four!" Jack's saying, and it does something in him, the way the kid was listening to what he said, shoot the boxes, shoot the corners, the ball going everywhere, rolling away, Jack running down the driveway, looking both ways before heading onto the quiet Stoneham street, Tommy twirling around in a circle in his Zdeno shirt.

Tommy hits one hard and it strikes Oak right in the center of his bruised chest. "Fuck."

"Sorry—" Tommy looks scared.

"You said fuck," Jack is laughing.

"Knock it off." Oak looks at Tommy, "That was a good shot, Tommy."

The kid looks at him, then down at his feet. "Thanks."

Arlene's in the doorway, watching.

Jack sees her. "Mum, look at this."

Jack slaps the five iron at the ball, clips it, the ball spinning sideways, the five-iron scraping the blacktop.

"That's Dad's club!" Tommy says, back to being a pain in the ass, Oak sees that the kid says it because he wants to bug her.

"Yeah," Arlene says and lights a cigarette.

"No smoking," Jack says.

Kyle's in the kitchen, watching from the window. Tommy drops his stick and walks past his mother into the house.

"Oak tree Zdeno!" Jack is saying. "No one can beat you. You could lift a horse!"

Oak looks at his sister, smoking, Jack coming over to him, tugging on his sweater.

"Couldn't you, Uncle Oak? Couldn't you lift a horse?"

"Maybe a pony," he tells the kid. Oak goes and stands with his sister.

"You see what I mean?" Arlene says, exhaling, watching Tommy go.

"He's all right."

"But they give things meaning, Tim. Children. Perspective."

Oak nods. Jack's twirling circles, his face up at the sky.

"Do you even sleep, Timmy?"

He kisses his sister's cheek. He goes and joins his nephew who's pretending to block shots in front of the empty net. He grabs a basketball that's lying on the grass and bounces it at his sister. "Let's go, Ma," he says.

"Nah, come on."

"Come on, Ma—" Jack says.

Arlene drops the butt to the flagstones, crushes it with her shoe. She dribbles out, dekes Oak right-left-right, goes in for a lay-up, fades back, and ices a floater. "Arrrlene O'Connor!" Oak announces, Jack running for the ball, Arlene smiling as she goes after Jack, Oak with his hands up for the pass, with Tommy and Kyle in the kitchen window watching.

31

Slats said to leave Only alone. Oak had to drag it out of Slats, but Slats gave him an address, a Georgian restaurant in Brighton, said Only was there most mornings.

And he is, Only's sitting there, at a table in the back, tan, fat, slick black hair, with two big Georgian guys, drinking coffee.

Only smiles when he sees him, opens his arms, stands, and extends his hand. "Oak, hello. Saba, Peter, this is Oak, a great skater."

Oak looks at Only's extended hand. The young guy is big, a tattoo on his neck. The old guy, Saba, is bigger. Oak doesn't care.

"So," Only lowers his hand. "This is business," Only says, like the guy hasn't ripped him off for four hundred bucks and snapped Esteban's back.

The old guy would be like punching a bull. Oak turns an angle on the guy, in case the guy feels like standing. The young guy's playing it cool, looking at his phone. Oak sees he's got a scar right across his eyelid.

"I just want my pay," he tells Only.

"Who is this guy?" the old guy says.

"He's not worth much," the young guy says, looking up.

Only's looking at him. "He's not worth much now, true. But he was, before, well I do not know, before what, Oak? What made you into what you have become?" Only nods his chin toward the entrance of the shop. "Let's walk."

Oak follows Only out to the sidewalk.

"What are you doing, Oak?" Only asks when they get outside.

"I want the money you owe me."

"So you will spend it on drugs?"

"No."

"Look at you."

"Four hundred."

"You didn't run?"

"Of course I fucking ran."

Only looks at him, like something is coming clear to Only.

"But you got no money?"

"What? No."

"You were supposed to get paid before, when you were told."

In his mind, Oak sees Zink running. He sees Slats running. He hears Slats telling him not to come to see Only, that he should just let it go. Zink running. Slats running. Then the police, when he and the rest were still up on the roof.

He feels the gas go from his legs. "Slats?"

"This was a setup on Ivan. I told you this. Let's say, the guy who did the job wants to be my rival. I sent a message. Slats knew."

Oak leans against the wall. He cannot imagine that Slats would have set him up. Maybe Slats didn't know. Maybe it was Zink. Although he can't see Zink setting them up, either.

Only puts a hand on Oak's shoulder. "I'm not going to ask Peter to come out here. Do you know, Oak, what Peter does?"

Only opens his coat, gets a billfold from his inside coat pocket, showing a gun in some kind of holder in his belt.

"That," Only glances at his gun, "Peter calls a pea shooter. Says it is for a woman."

Only opens his billfold, counts out four fifties. "We'll call things level, okay?"

Oak takes the money.

"And for the future, be more careful about these behaviors." Only does up his coat. "There is always something, someone, bigger and stronger. Mightier even than you, Oak." Only shrugs. "Or me." Only's eyes narrow. "I have a thought," Only says. "I'm thinking you will do a job for me alone?"

"You broke my friend's neck."

"The Mexican's?" Only shakes his head. "They do work they are not qualified to do. They want money. They take the chance. I don't design the world."

"What's the job?"

"You drive a truck, make a delivery."

"Drugs."

"No."

"Why not your boy Slats?"

"Slats is not my boy. You drive the truck from Lynn to Providence. I understand you skated in Providence."

Oak looks at Only. He takes a breath against the gripping inside his guts and head.

"If you don't know, then you don't know," Only says. "The owner of the truck, he's Chinese. *He* doesn't know. Only Saba knows. And that's why Saba does not drive."

"The kid inside with the eye?"

"Never. He is an idiot. No, not an idiot, but not for a job like this. He is not a bull. You are a bull."

"How much?"

"Five hundred dollars. But you can ask for seven. Go ahead. That is good business. I think Saba will agree to say yes."

Eight days until Worcester. He's going to need to money to see Barry again.

"Yes."

Oak walks with Only back inside the cafe.

32

Kip is asleep in the car. Oak's got WEEI on. The hockey guy, Don, is a moron. Don's talking about how one of the Bruins, a Bruin Oak's never heard of, was stinking up the rink. Saying how the guy can't skate anymore, how the guy is scared to hit. Like Don's ever played. Everyone's an expert. Never mind good fortune or luck. Who your line mates are, who you skate against and when. How you're treated on the bus. They had a goalie, "The Truth," in North Carolina, who never partied and was always reading his Bible. Oak didn't care, he liked the guy, played cards with him, plus every goalie he ever met was whacked, all goalies are whacked, but the other guys were on The Truth all the time. Put porn in his Bible. Sent a hooker to his room. The Truth was gone in six weeks, his goals against average up two clicks because of his treatment on the bus. So you never knew. What Oak does know is that the Bruin he's never even heard of can skate a fuck of a lot better than Don on the radio. *Go fuck yourself, Don,* he thinks. *Go. Fuck. Yourself.*

Oak shuts it off and smacks the dash. Fucking Slats. He doesn't know for sure. He can't imagine Slats doing him like that.

He's thinking, again, how Slats and Zink were downstairs at the building site, how they might have seen the police cars before he did up on the roof. Or Zink might have told Slats and not him. It might be Rob Zink. Oak doesn't know Rob Zink well. But Slats knew Only. Slats knew Zink. Slats brought them together. Slats.

When Oak called, Slats didn't answer his phone. Or when he called again.

"Hey!" Kip hollers himself awake. For a minute, Kip looks like a boy, with his curly hair and hoodie, looking at Oak like he doesn't know where he is. "What the fuck?" Kip says.

Oak can see the vein in Kip's neck beating fast from the dream.

THEY KNOCK ON JOAN'S DOOR. The wreath's up. When there's no answer, Oak rings the bell. Nothing.

He tries the door handle. It's open. Unlocked. He sticks his head in.

"Joan?"

They stand in her foyer. It's 10:00 a.m. She might be sleeping. She might have forgotten he was coming. Oak goes into the kitchen. On the table, beside an ashtray full of smokes, there's an opened file folder filled with the photos of him that she took. He looks wrecked.

And there are more photos of the cop he decked, too. The cop's eyes are blackened, his nose is taped up. Oak remembers that other lawyer talking about how the cop has a baby at home. Oak doesn't know if the lawyer was bullshitting or not. He flips the folder over. Kip doesn't need to see it. Oak doesn't need the kid's questions.

Out the kitchen window, Oak sees Joan standing in her backyard. He's not sure she's not dreaming, sleepwalking. He doesn't want to scare her. He watches her through the glass. She's standing there, in a green robe, smoking, looking at the dead, dried-up tree.

"Wait here," he tells Kip back in the foyer.

Oak goes around to the backyard and stands beside her.

"We had birds in that tree," she says, like they've been talking. "Charles built a contraption to keep the squirrels away. And then the tree died. Two years ago. All at once. The birds never came back."

"It's winter." He says it careful.

She's just standing there, her hair all over her face and sticking-out ears and long neck, her eyes dark-circled, barefoot on the wet, cold ground.

"You want to go inside, Joan?"

"I just want to finish this cigarette." She exhales. "I didn't know if you'd be coming."

"I didn't know if you'd want me to."

Behind her, the backyard is reflected in the husband's window. She's not looking at him. She's looking at the tree.

"Where did you learn how to dance?"

"My parents. My father really."

"Mine played ping pong."

"He's gone?"

"Dead. Yeah."

She keeps looking at the tree.

"Why did you punch out the cop?"

"I don't know."

"You have a daughter."

"Yeah?"

"You see her?"

"Yeah, I see her."

She nods. "Your friend Kevin Slattery adopted her," she says.

He doesn't know what's happening.

"Yes."

"I don't pray, Tim. I don't . . . have hobbies." She flips her cigarette at the tree. "We worked. Charles and I."

"I can cut that tree down for you. The dead one."

"I've been meaning to call someone. Charlie . . . said he'd do it. But I knew we'd have to call someone."

"You got a chainsaw?" Oak grinds out her cigarette with his boot.

She shakes her head.

"You got a neighbor with a chainsaw?"

She shrugs.

"It's all right. I can get one. No problem. If it doesn't have bugs, the tree, you'll get some firewood out of it."

"It does have bugs. That's why it died."

"I'll get a chipper, too, then."

She's suddenly loud. "Why are you *helping* me?"

He stops. The yard becomes very bright. Like he's taken a sharp hit to the head. "Why are you helping *me*?"

"To piss off my parents."

Oak laughs. It's as good a reason as any. "You're a rebel?"

Joan shakes her head. "Whatever the opposite of that is, Tim."

INSIDE, KIP'S IN THE DINING ROOM, opening the cans of paint.

"Hi, Kip," Joan says, steady, the Joan in the backyard a ghost now, though he's not sure this one isn't more so. "There's a shirt there for you if you want it, so you don't get covered in paint."

It's a man's shirt. She's hung it on a chair in the dining room. Her husband's shirt.

Oak skated with a guy in Michigan, the guy was in the army reserves and he got called out. The Afghans blew his arm off. When he got back, the guy posted how he could still feel his arm even though it was now Afghan dirt. Oak sees her ghost-bowling. He sees her ghost-standing in her yard.

Kip gets his sweater off.

"Oh, Kip—" Joan says.

Kip's arms are black and blue.

Oak looks at Joan. "Nice friends he's got, huh?"

Kip's face goes hot, like he forgot the bruises were there. Kip quickly slips into the husband's shirt. "I can handle it," Kip says.

"Can you handle painting?" Oak says. "I got to do some yard work."

OAK GOES TO TWO NEIGHBORING HOUSES. The second guy has a chainsaw. Gives it over like that. Brookline—no doubt the guy bought it himself.

It's not much of a tree, ten feet maybe, it makes a straight drop across the yard. It's wood ants as far as Oak can see. He hacks away the buggy parts. He's never used a chainsaw. It doesn't take long until he's okay with it, carving through the wood. He makes an animal from a branch, sort of a rabbit. Slices its head off.

His T-shirt sticks to his scabs. He can feel them, hot and wet, he doesn't want the blood to get onto his good shirt when he puts it back on, and he doesn't want his painting shirt to get covered in wood. He takes his T-shirt off, hangs it on the fence. The cold air feels good on his skin. He tears back into what's left of the tree. Joan can have firewood, sticks anyway, he's thinking, from the dry wood. He can pile it for her in her garage.

That'd be nice, to have a fireplace. They had one, but it was or-namental, filled in with bricks. When Oak turns to look for the chimney, because he's pretty sure he saw a fireplace in her living room, he sees Joan in the kitchen, in the picture window by the sink, watching him.

He feels himself, shirtless in the cold, with his scars and open cuts, his black and yellow bruises. He turns his back to her, wipes the sweat and sawdust from his face with his arm.

Charlie. A scientist. A professor. Running, thinking, a smart guy, really smart, the old equipment, Joan coming home to talk about her pro bono cases, good work on behalf of good people, wine with dinner, the fire. Charlie should have chopped this wood. Charlie should have stacked it for her. Charlie should have fixed the arbor and planted flowers for her in the yard.

Later, the guy was thinking. Later.

Oak's phone rings. He checks back over his shoulder. She's gone. Oak shuts the chainsaw down, leans it on the stump. Number unknown. It's not Slats.

"Hello, Oak, this is Saba."

A cardinal loops around where the treetop used to be.

"Are you there, Oak?"

"Yeah."

"Your delivery is confirmed. You will find the documentation in the glove box. Should you need it."

"The documentation?"

"In the glove box. Take care, Oak."

The line goes dead.

He calls Slats for a third time. No answer. "I need to talk with you, Slats," Oak says, again. With every unreturned call, Oak feels him and Slats falling into some kind of black void. The cardinal lands on a telephone wire that runs from the street to the house next door. Another bird joins it. They sit there.

Oak picks up the chainsaw and rips back into the dead tree, closing his eyes against the spray.

KIP'S MOVING FURNITURE IN THE LIVING ROOM when Oak comes back inside. On the mantel above her fireplace there are pictures and a smiling Buddha and a cross of St. John's. The living room is the same job as the dining room, two rollers and two brushes and keeping the drip on the drop cloth. They paint a while.

"So, what happened, anyway, with your mother?" Kip asks suddenly, looking at the wall.

"She got old." Oak's shoulder hurts from the chainsaw, which isn't, he thinks, a good sign. He's got pills in his pocket. He carries them around in case he needs them.

"Did you like her?"

"She was my mother. You like yours?"

Kip doesn't say anything.

"Did you?"

Kip says something quiet that sounds like yeah.

"What?"

"Yes," Kip says louder.

Oak nods. "What's this song?" he asks.

"I don't know. It sucks though. Some jazz is good. Some sucks. My father says bad jazz is like chickens fighting in the back of the bodega."

"What are you anyway, Puerto Rican?"

"My mother was white."

"Hey, I don't care."

"Why'd you ask then?"

"Just curious. You got a head of hair on you."

"She died of cancer," Kip says, painting.

"Mine too."

Oak picks up the roller. They paint.

"This is Herbie Hancock, I think," Kip says when a new song starts. "We got one piano at school. I go in early. There's a priest who gives me lessons for nothing. And my father buys me lessons when he can."

"I used to skate midnight and first thing in the morning. Before the sun was even up. My old man would drive me."

"That's cool."

"Not if you like sleeping."

"Sleeping's for the dead," Kip says, like Oak told Arlene. "I had a dream that I died. My teacher said if you have a dream that you die, you're dead, but I woke up and went to school."

"Zombie."

"Yeah." Kip smiles. "If I was a zombie, I wouldn't eat people. I'd make them think I was going to eat them, and make them give me money and shit. I'd eat pizza. I'd walk into you know, Papa Gino's and be like, aaaaaarrrrr."

"Pizza Zombie of Quincy Center."

"Why you get into hockey anyway?"

"I don't know. I just started . . . Why you play the piano?"

"I like it."

Oak nods. Goes into the kitchen. Opens the pills. Gets out an Oxy. Cups the pill and some water into his mouth. Shoves the bottle back into his jacket that's hanging on the kitchen chair so they won't rattle around when he's painting.

"What's up?" Kip says from the living room.

"Nothing." He doesn't hear Joan. He thinks of her watching him from the kitchen window. The way she was just standing in the yard when he got there spooks him.

Oak goes up the stairs. "Joan?" he calls out. She doesn't answer. At the top of the stairs, he sees her in her office in front of her computer, with headphones on. The door is open. He's trying to think of something to say. He's going to turn around and not bother her when he sees himself on her computer screen, knocking some goon over the bench boards on hockeyfight.com. He gets into her doorway. He remembers the fight. It was from last season, in Texas. The guy was a bender from Alberta, they called him Big Chief because of his tomahawk. Oak got a massive hit on him. Timed it, flipped Big Chief over his own bench boards. On-screen, Oak stands in front of the visitor's bench, his face bleeding, staring down Big Chief, whose nose he busted, waiting to see if the guy wants back on the ice. Oak watches himself skate to the penalty box for ten minutes of rest. He doesn't remember hearing the fans, but on Joan's computer he sees them going crazy.

He wants to tell her how the guy did his lineman in. How he didn't have a choice, he had to reestablish himself, let Major and his team and the leagues know that he still had real game. But he doesn't say anything. If she hasn't seen McDonald yet, he thinks, she will.

Joan clicks off. A legal document fills her screen. Joan rests her chin in the palm of her hand, staring at it.

He should turn and go back downstairs. Instead, he knocks on her opened door. She turns and takes off her headphones. Her expression is blank.

"So you've seen all that shit," Oak says.

She nods. "I've watched it before."

"You know about what happened in Albuquerque?"

"Yes."

"You saw it?"

"It's not hard to find."

The screensaver comes on. It's her and Charles on a river. They're young.

"Why do you fight?" she says, across the room from him.

He starts to say that it's part of the game. He starts to say how he has to protect his snipers. He starts to tell her that it's the only way he can get real ice time back so he won't have to fight. But no words come. "I don't know," he finally says.

"Charlie didn't fight. He was always smiling." She closes her laptop. "I don't have any idea what he was feeling."

He wants to get out of the room. He stands there instead. "I took the tree down."

"I saw. Thank you."

"There were a couple of birds. Like they're waiting to come back."

Joan doesn't say anything.

Oak nods. "Okay." He goes down the stairs. He stands for a while in the empty front hall. He feels the Oxy work against his racing heart.

"Mingus Mingus Mingus Mingus Mingus!" Kip calls out from the living room, cranking up the Bose.

33

They've got the living room nearly done. The sun's down. Joan comes back in from wherever she's been. Oak heard her come down the stairs and leave.

She's carrying Chinese food. "I brought dinner."

He realizes, again, how kind she looks, coming into the kitchen, unpacking the food on the kitchen table, with what she must be feeling, with what she saw.

"You better call your father, Kip," Joan says. "You can use my phone."

Kip's tapping his fingers along the window glass. A wintry rain blows against it.

"Kip?" she says.

Kip turns. Oak sees that Kip's face is beading with sweat. Kip takes Joan's phone into the living room.

Oak gets the food from the bags. "You didn't need to do this."

"You've got to eat."

"What about you? You got no food in your fridge."

"I eat," she says. She gets bowls. Oak hears Kip talking to his father in the next room.

"I'm sorry about what you saw."

"Tim. I've seen a lot worse."

She pushes a bowl of rice toward him. "What was Texas like?" she asks.

"The hockey?"

"No. Other things."

"It's not like around here. You can walk a straight line into the desert, and there's birds you've never seen, and cactus, and jack rabbits with big ears, and prairie dogs and snakes."

"I don't need snakes."

"The sky stretches out so that you don't have to see anything close-up. Your mind can sort of let go and relax."

She's looking at him.

"The fans throw tortillas on the ice."

She laughs.

Kip comes back. "Let's do it!" Kip says loud. "But first, ladies and gentlemen—" Kip lunges to her piano, plays a furious tune, not good, in the end he pounds the keys with his fists and elbows, then does his fingers along the keys like Jerry Lee Lewis.

Joan's smiling, but it's a polite smile.

"Dudes, let's eat!"

Kip lurches to the table, piles noodles into a bowl. Then he says, "I'm gonna take mine outside."

"It's raining," Joan says.

Kip grabs his bowl and goes out the front door. They hear it slam.

"His father probably told him to get his ass home," Oak says.

There's the jazz music from the radio and the rain against the kitchen windows. She puts a silver set of chopsticks beside him.

"Special Korean sets from my mother."

"Kim is Korean, right?"

"We do eat Chinese food, if that's what you were thinking."

"I was."

She shakes her head, smiles a little. "I've lived here longer than you have, Tim. Thirty-eight years. My grandparents are from Seoul, though."

His great-grandparents, both sides, came over during the famine like half of South Boston.

"They leave during the war?"

"World War II. My grandfather was a professor. And my father was a professor."

"And then you married a professor."

She looks at him steadily. "Yes."

"I'm sorry."

"It's okay. It's true. I married a professor. Charlie was a physicist. Nuclear physics. And I became a lawyer and my sister who you met had a family and my other sister became a K-Pop Californian without the talent and here we are."

When she talks, he feels calmer. When he thinks about her dead husband's office, the bed, him balling on her computer, he wants to smack something. Death, if he could find it.

He can't use the chopsticks, even if he was good at them. "I probably better use a fork. I'm sorry." He tears open the plastic utensil bag. "You run?" he asks. "I saw the shoes by the door."

"We were doing a biathlon."

"You gotta run. Bike. Something. You can't sit around."

"It makes you crazy," she says.

"Yeah."

"Crazy."

"We could go skating."

She looks at him. Shakes her head. "Where do you come from?" she says quietly.

"Southie."

She gathers the empty containers and takes them to the trash. She's barely eaten. Her back is to him. "The cop you punched is still on medical leave," she says. She steps on the pedal of the trash can. "There's no squad car tape. That helps us. Means they didn't turn it on, means they didn't *want* to turn it on."

"Does he really have a baby at home?"

Joan turns to look at him. Past her, out the window, Oak sees Kip in the backyard with the chainsaw up over his head. In an instant, Kip gets the chainsaw going and lashes into a standing tree.

"Fuck." Oak jumps to his feet.

"Tim?"

Oak rushes past Joan and out to the backyard. Kip's standing in a spray of wood, ripping into another tree. Oak grabs Kip by the shoulder. "What the fuck are you doing?"

Kip's laughing. His eyes are slits, his pupils balling inside them. Oak puts it together. Kip's gone into Oak's jacket pocket and eaten the husband's pills.

"Turn that off," Oak yells. "Now."

Kip whirls to face him, holding the chain saw out in front. "Lightsaber!"

Oak leaps back. Joan's calling from the doorway. The kid's speeding like a train.

Oak nods gently, though he wants to snap the kid in two. Kip waves the chainsaw in the wet air. He whirls and digs the blade back into the bark, the blade bouncing back at him.

Oak lets Kip cut for a second, and then jumps him and gets his arms around Kip from behind, his hands smothering Kip's on the chainsaw, holding the blade away from Kip's body. Oak's face is squeezed to the side of Kip's head. "Let it go," Oak says. He bends Kip's fingers from the trigger, the blade bouncing wildly against the tree. "Let it go, Kip," Oak says, directly into Kip's ear.

"You don't tell me what to do," Kip yells, the blade roaring.

"Let go, Kip—" Oak can't get into position.

"Fuck you. You don't tell me what to do."

"LET GO." Oak tries to spin him, but the chainsaw only slices downward, inches from Kip's own legs.

Kip thrashes in Oak's clench, the blade sawing air. Oak's face is crushing against Kip's ear.

"KIP—"

"NO!"

He Tysons it. Kip screams.

The safety catches.

"You bit my fucking ear!"

Oak smacks the chainsaw from Kip's hand to the grass. He picks Kip up with one arm and carries the boy toward the house. Joan screams when she sees Kip's bleeding ear.

"You're out of your fucking head, Kip."

"Fuck you—"

"How many did you take?"

"Leave me the fuck alone. My fucking ear!" Kip's swooning, seeing his own blood.

"Here," Joan says, in the foyer, and Oak sees how scared she is. She's got a wet washcloth.

"He took your husband's drugs," Oak says.

"*He* took them," Kip says. "He bit my ear off. He's a fucking animal."

Oak keeps his arms around Kip. Joan presses the wet cloth to Kip's ear. Kip yowls.

"We've got to take him to the emergency room," Joan says.

Oak nods. And suddenly, Kip is slack. Oak lowers him gently to her kitchen floor. He keeps his arms loosely around the kid, kneeling.

"How many pills did you take?"

"However many *you* left."

"You want your stomach pumped?"

"One of each."

Oak nods. The morphine is going to fuck the kid up, but he'll be all right, all 120 pounds of him.

"We've got to go get your ear bandaged up," Oak says.

"You bit me," Kip says quietly. "You fucking bit me."

"Let me see your phone," he says to Joan.

"I can call," she says.

"Just give me the fucking phone, Joan."

He's putting more together. She gives him her phone.

He swipes to the last outgoing call. It's from over an hour ago. He shows it carefully to Joan. "You know this number?"

"I think it's the Chinese place?"

She's scared now and a part of him feels sorry he's snapped at her, but that part is crushed by the other parts that are storming.

Oak presses Send. After a ring, it is the Chinese place.

It's not Kip's father.

Oak hangs up.

He looks at the kid.

34

He's not taking Kip to the emergency room. The hospital will see how drugged up Kip is and there'll be bad questions.

He drives to Shark's gym.

Shark's in the ring, with a kid, holding pads. The kid's Kip's age, and big, and he's hitting large, PAL T-shirt, a couple guys in their twenties watching, and Oak knows all Shark is telling the kid is to breath.

Shark looks over. Gets one of the twenty-year-olds to take the pads.

They get inside Shark's office.

"What's going on?"

"His ear."

"He bit me."

Shark looks at Oak hard. "I don't need a mess, Oak." To Kip, "If he bit you, why you standing here next to him?"

"He won't let me go."

Shark looks hard at Kip. Kip goes quiet.

"Let me see your ear." Shark gets the hair out of the way. Shark's leaning down so his face is right there for Kip. "This boy on something?"

"Yeah."

Shark nods. Says to Kip, "I'm gonna fix your ear."

Kip doesn't say anything.

"He got a mother?"

Oak shakes his head no.

Shark gets his box. Puts Kip in his desk chair.

A couple fighters stand in the doorway. "You want something?" Shark says, and they go.

Shark soaks a cloth in alcohol and squeezes it fast to Kip's torn-up ear.

Kip goes rigid, "Fuck!" But Shark's got a heavy arm roped around his shoulders.

"So you do talk. And nasty, too." Shark leans in again to look Kip in the eyes. "Watch it."

But Kip's eyes are gone.

"He took some shit," Oak starts to say.

"I don't want to hear about it, Tim. All right," Shark says to Kip, "this is going to hurt like a dog bite but then you'll be all done."

Oak knows what's coming, remembers it, Shark's formula, tonic, Shark calls it, he'd dump it on bloody cuts, rub it into blue knots, shove it on a Q-tip up his professional fighters' noses.

But this time, when Shark squeezes the brown tonic onto Kip's ear, Kip doesn't make a sound. "You're tough." Shark butterflies the ear. "He should be okay without stitches. Who's he live with?"

"His old man."

Shark nods. "Tell him to take him in in the morning if it's still bleeding."

"Thanks, Shark."

Shark carefully repacks his kit. He doesn't look at Oak. "All right, Tim."

35

They've got to wait it out. The ear will heal. Oak's seen worse. The drugs will wear off. Oak takes him to Atomic Burger.

They get in a booth, Kip still pressing Joan's washcloth to his butterflied ear. Oak realizes he should have gotten an ice pack from Shark.

"Stay there," Oak says.

Oak goes to the counter. "You got a cup of ice?"

The girl looks at him, gets him his ice.

Oak comes back to the booth, fills the bloody washcloth.

Kip is swaying in his seat.

"Lean against that wall and hold that to your ear."

Kip does.

"Look. I know you know I took some pills. Look at me. You don't want to turn out like me."

"That's for fucking sure."

There's a family, a father maybe his age with three kids, looking at them.

"What do you want to eat?"

Kip doesn't say anything, his eyes are closing.

"Hey—" Oak slaps the table.

Kip's eyes snap open.

"Just sit here."

Oak goes back to the counter, orders two cheeseburgers, two fish fillets, and two large Cokes.

The place is crowded, and people are looking at them. The guy, there with his family, keeps glancing over at Kip, then back at Oak at the counter. Guy wears a BC jacket, like he's eighteen. Fat Irish face. Oak turns to him. "Mind your own fucking business."

"I got kids here," the guy says.

Oak waits for the girl to get his food on the tray. Thinks about the phone numbers on Joan's phone and his. Takes a long, hard breath. Blows it out.

He carries the food back to the booth. Unwraps a burger and fish sandwich for Kip. French fries. Puts them in front of him with the Coke. Kip won't want to eat, but just in case he does.

"You hungry?"

Kip shakes his head.

"Drink something. Here—" He gets the straw into the Coke for him. Kip's leaning his head against the wall.

"So," Oak says it as steady as he can, "who did you in?"

Kip keeps looking at nothing, the ceiling lights bouncing against the wall.

"You stand up for yourself?"

Nothing.

"When you took your shirt off to paint," Oak says it as steady as he can. "That's not from those boys."

"I just want to go home," Kips says quietly. His face is greasy with sweat. "I want to go home."

"Why isn't your father's number on my phone? On Joan's phone?"

"What—"

It's the wrong time to leap on the kid like this. It's only because he's only now maybe figuring the shit out: the bruises, the fake phone calls. He's going to rip someone's head off if he doesn't talk about it right now. "You made like you were calling your father. Twice. Last week in Joan's driveway. His number doesn't show up on my phone. Today in her living room. His number doesn't show up on her phone."

"Fuck off."

"Look at me."

"I said fuck off." Kip stares at the untouched burger.

Oak feels his own heart squeeze inside his chest. "Do you stand up to him?"

He's trying to breathe steady.

Kip twirls his plastic silverware.

"Do you?"

"I said fuck off."

Oak leans down until his chin is almost on the table to see Kip's eyes.

"Next time, you call me. You've got my number. You got to be the hammer, Kip, not the nail."

Kip's knocking the plastic salt and pepper shakers together.

"You understand me, Kip? It's fucked up, being a man."

Kip pushes up from the table. "Excuse me," he says fast, suddenly polite like a child. Kip falls toward the bathroom. Oak follows after to find the kid puking in the bathroom stalls.

Oak waits. He wets a couple paper towels with cold water. A runt, fourteen going on eleven, an A-bomb tearing at his guts and brain.

When Kip comes out of the stall, Kip's crying.

"Yeah," Oak says. Kip sort of falls against the tiles near the hand blower. The machine goes on. Kip leans there, his hair dancing.

"You're okay now," Oak says. "You puked it out. You're okay."

Kip doesn't say anything. Oak wipes the puke off him, gets an arm around his shoulders. "Let's get out of here." Oak straight-arms the men's room door.

On the way out, the BC guy is laughing with his kids, one kid telling some kind of story, the kid's arms waving over his head, his father clapping his hands.

THEY SIT IN HIS MOTHER'S CAR. Kip's a black twig in a black night, his face against the window against his folded hand. The heater is on, the radio low. Oak lets him sleep. He's got a Jack pint tucked in the car door's pocket. Oak drinks some, pours some on his bleeding knuckles. One time his father took him to a Bruins game. After, they went to Atomic Burger. There was another guy sitting with his son who didn't like the way Oak had beat his kid a few weeks earlier in the ring. The guy started talking crap, right out loud, in front of his son, about Oak's old man. How he was a drunk. How he didn't teach Oak right from wrong. Oak was eleven, he'd just started fighting, and he remembers the fight with the kid because Shark had always taught him to punch through the bell, to punch until the ref stands in your face, and he had punched that kid to the ropes and he had kept punching, waiting for the ref or the bell, and that was the first time he'd seen a face burst with blood, the nose becoming not a nose but something else. And he remembers his anger, his rage, that the kid's nose would do that, that the kid would just hang moaning against the ropes, and Oak remembers feeling he had to beat the weakness out of the kid until finally they had to lift the kid from the concrete floor after a hook from Oak sent the kid over the ropes.

At Atomic, he waited for his father to take the guy on.

"Take off your jersey," his father said. His father had bought him a Terry O'Reilly vintage jersey that he'd put on over his own shirt as soon as he got it. Oak thought he was going to have to fight the kid again, this time without helmets, and he didn't want to but he was ready. He took off the jersey. "Now go give it to him." Oak remembers being confused, his father's voice was flat, his father's eyes were slits, his face was drunk hot but steady.

Oak went over with the Terry O'Reilly jersey that his old man had spent sixty dollars on, that he'd really wanted, and gave it to the kid. "Here," he said. The kid didn't want it, Oak could tell, but at the same time he must have felt like Oak did, like, what the fuck is going on? So the kid took it, and the kid's father sat there and shut up.

When they left, they found the jersey thrown down in the slushy parking lot, right where they would see it. "Pick it up," his father said.

"I don't want it."

"Yes, you do."

Oak picked up the jersey and took it home.

OAK WALKS KIP TO THE DOOR AT 1:00 A.M. Helps him get his key in the lock. Oak realizes he doesn't know anything, for certain, about Kip's old man: he wouldn't have called his own father either half the time, or his ma, but his old man never laid a hand on him but for a couple of times when he deserved it. Inside, the house is neat. Oak gets the hall light on. Looks in the front room. LPs line the walls, it's like a record library, any open wall space is crowded with records and framed photographs.

Oak sees Kip's father asleep on the living room sofa.

"He got sick," Oak says to the guy. "I should've called you."

Kip's father doesn't move. He's skinny, shirtless, lying there like he's sleeping but his eyes are open. Junkie eyes. Oak tries to catch Kip's eyes, but Kip is leaning against the railing of the stairs. "I'm sorry," Oak says, and the guy doesn't move, Kip heading up the stairs, and before Oak closes the door behind him he looks at Kip's father, long, a warning, until he knows for certain the guy's seen it.

36

Shark's watching him as he comes back in the office, in the morning, when Oak's not supposed to be there. The gym's full up.

It's like they're still talking from the night before.

"A hundred thousand people used to go see a boxing match, Oak," Shark says. "Dempsey–Tunney. I saw Floyd Patterson when I was a boy, and he let us do chin-ups on his arm. Tyson–Holyfield. My brother Smooth used to say, you marry the ring, boxing is your family. That's why I only went in part-time. Kept my job with the T. Went home nights. You prepare a fighter, you do Dundee's slow growth, you do the fundamentals, you get him keen, you get him right, you are in true, you understand, Tim? And then, well, you know this, he flashes a look into the blackout, he poses a punch, he forgets one small thing, or maybe he doesn't even do nothing, he doesn't do nothing wrong, but he's still wrong, and he loses. Despite all that prep and love."

Shark shakes his head.

"I'm sorry. I didn't sleep last night. I got to decide what to do about this place. I'll be sixty-two in a year, retire age. I don't know if a boxing gym is what people want anymore. I can just go down to Florida. Play the dogs."

"You'd hate Florida."

"God's waiting room. I know it. Shit."

Shark looks out toward the gym.

"Don't get old, Oak, it's not suitable."

They laugh. That's the kind of things Shark always said. Not suitable.

"How's the boy?"

"Okay."

"What went on?"

"Stupidity."

Shark nods. "You get him home?"

"Yeah."

Shark's quiet for a moment. Oak feels like he's rushing forward although he's standing still. He sat by the fort when the sun came up, drank a coffee to wake up his head. He saw her, when she was four, and he was home the first Christmas from Grand Rapids. They brought her to the house, his ma with presents, a knit hat, some plastic horses. He didn't know what to get her. He brought her dolls that fit inside each other, each one a girl skating, and you could spin them and the girl would twirl around. Him and Shannon and his ma. He played horses with Kate on the living room floor.

"I appreciate the way you did the office, Oak. Even dusted the trophies I see. And the photographs."

"I need you to cut my hair, Shark."

Shark is quiet, then. "It's been a while since I cut anyone's hair, Oak. Why should I cut yours? You don't even take my trash out. Or make my coffee."

"Will you just do it?"

"I don't have my shears. Or my razor. All I got is maybe clippers and comb."

They look at each other. The photos and the trophies, the serenity prayer, thirteen, fourteen, fifteen.

"You meet a girl?" Shark tries to joke.

Oak doesn't answer.

Shark closes his eyes. Opens them. "Okay. I know it. I know it. All right." Shark hands Oak a coffee mug. "Put another motherfucking pot on, Tim, and let me find my scissors."

Shark used to cut everyone's hair right in the gym. Him, all the fighters. Later, his ma got into it, too, setting up in their den, the girls in there smoking, playing old Dexy's Midnight Runners and Sade. Oak changes Shark's coffee filter. Dumps in some Maxwell House. Pours water into the back of the machine.

"You want a Southie buzz cut, right? Marky Mark?"

Oak smiles for Shark. Oak sits in Shark's chair. Shark tucks a towel into Oak's sweatshirt, drapes a bigger one around Oak's shoulders. He starts to cut. Oak knows his scalp is banged up, with scabs and scars, but Shark doesn't say anything. Shark's hands smell of cigarettes and soap.

"I could do your beard, too, you want. Even it out."

"Sure."

"Marla used to want me to cut her hair," Shark says, talking about his wife. "But I wouldn't do it. A man shouldn't cut his wife's hair. Angie's neither. Just the boys in the gym. My brother Smooth would never let me touch him after a time. You remember that head of hair on him? It was a magnet to the ladies. Do you know, Tim, he died in bed with a lady I'd never even heard him talk about? She was bringing him breakfast and he was dead. Marla, too, she died right beside me. Only just turned sixty." Shark pauses, then starts cutting again. "We're young people, Oak, to be this old."

Oak's hair falls into his lap.

"Angie, though, she's still young, my daughter out there doing her thing, out there in San Francisco in a big job. That's Angie. Doing okay. I'd like to get out there, to the Bay area, I only been once and that was before she was born."

It's pretty fast, the crying. It just comes on him, Oak feeling his eyes pouring out tears.

Shark doesn't say anything, until the tears are running into his beard, Oak can feel it, he has to wipe his face with his sleeve.

"I'm gonna make you look good, Tim," Shark says.

Oak can't stop crying.

"You'll hold your head up. I'm going to make you look good." Shark runs a hand through Oak's hair. "That daughter of yours, she'll know. You're all right."

"I think I fucked it all up, Shark."

"Nah." Shark wipes at his own face with his sleeve. "You're good."

37

Oak waits in the cold Revere beach parking lot, standing by the seawall. Kate wanted to meet him at the beach. He took the T up, then walked, the sky December gray, the water black, white, purple behind him on the rocks. He bought her a green Irish sweater that he hopes she'll like. He holds the sweater in a bag.

A smashed-up Volvo pulls into the lot. It's an old guy and his dog, the dog running circles in the back, leaping out, the guy not even bothering with the leash, the dog charging the beach steps, the guy following, throwing a ball for the dog into the water.

Another car pulls in: a van, two workers eating lunch.

When Shannon's car pulls into the lot, Oak doesn't know where to look. When they see him, Shannon waves, and he smiles because she does.

Shannon rolls down her window. "Hi, Tim." Kate is looking straight ahead. He feels himself smile again. "Hi, Shannon. Hey, Kate."

Kate keeps looking at the water. Oak has to catch his breath, to keep steady, his guts pounding up in his throat.

"Kate," Shannon says.

He's standing there. Kate still doesn't look at him. She gets out of the car. "You want to walk on the beach a little?"

Kate turns and she looks at him now, and he sees her face, the sweetness of her, he wants to hold on to her but he knows what he's put there between them, that the distance is because of him. "Hi, Tim," she says.

He smiles. "Hi, Kate."

"This is a good beach to come to," she says. "Even when it's cold."

"Okay."

They get down the steps. She's wearing Doc Marten boots, black tights, a black skirt, but a regular hoodie, Holy Cross green, over a sweater, so that's good, she'll wear a sweater, he's holding the cardigan he got her in the bag.

"You got blue hair."

"Yeah."

"I like it."

She nods. "Mom made me wait until I was fourteen."

Her birthday. The day she was born. Skating in Maine. The last birthday, no, the one before that, he'd sent her a card. Maybe not even then. Before. He doesn't know what to say. How to be the father standing on the cold beach in the bright sun. "Here—"

Kate takes the bag from him.

"I figure it can keep you warm."

"Hot legs," Kate says and she laughs. "Mom was pissed when you left the funeral."

"Yeah, well. I probably should have stayed."

"But you couldn't. Right?"

He wipes his nose with his jacket sleeve. She lifts the sweater from the bag. The wind catches the bag, rattling it in her hand.

"I know I haven't been around, Kate. I've wanted to. It's just, I've always had games and jobs."

It's a plain green sweater. He thought it looked good. He found it at one of the new places on East Broadway. She's looking at it.

"But I wish I could have been around, like maybe I can be now. There's a team in Worcester."

She's looking at the sweater like she doesn't like it. She half turns from him, says something toward the dark water. Finally, and suddenly, she shoves the sweater back into the plastic bag. "You don't know me," she says.

He's standing there.

"You don't know me." She says it louder. "You don't know me," and she turns to him, the look that haunts him immediately, goes into his marrow, and she throws the bag with the sweater to his feet. Kate hurries up the metal steps to the car.

Shannon opens the door for her, their daughter collapsing into the passenger seat, enraged, Oak can see Kate screaming at her mother. And then Kate's quiet, and through the windshield glass he sees his daughter crying, her red hair, her blue hair, her green eyes, her heart-shaped face. For a minute they sit there, and then the car pulls backward, and Kate glances at him, a flash, her bangs on her forehead and stuck in her eyes, the moment bends time, before they drive away.

Oak watches the car disappear. He picks up the sweater. He puts it in the trash can by the steps.

38

The night before the Worcester tryout, he's dreaming while awake. Skating, he sees the patterns, cage, net, the goaltender slow across the goalmouth, Oak fast at him, smooth, clear, knowing every move the dude is going to make. Providence College Friars, St. Anthony Saints, Murphy rink, Quincy rink, Harvard rink and the Donato boys, the PC fans screaming, his ma and his sister pounding the glass, peewees bang!, midgets bang!, bantam bang! Ice block heaters in Michigan, crappies and walleyes, flash-poppers in the stands, Texas water heat rising, ice-steam, sweat-heavy bag skate, sweat-heavy gear. Oak's skating in a corner get-and-go, elbow to the soft ribs, the boys from Tabor Academy fold, the boys from Boston College fold, St. Lawrence College and Colgate, the pretty skaters from BU, have a handful of Chiclets and bounce. Goalmouth, slew foot, top shelf, glove side, stick side, bonfires on Wrightsville Beach, puking in the Carolina sand, puking in his truck, the hard punch to win the New England Silver Mittens, *hey, hey Southie Pride*, shot to the body, shot to the head, uppercut, hook. Sharkey cutting his hair. The goalie's coming out.

Oak knows what the guy doesn't know he's going to do, what the guy's trying to avoid, deke left, his tooth in the flesh of some goon's hand, a needle full of Prednisone, deke right, a needle full of Toradol, blue line, red line, *MVP, MVP, MVP*, the rink funneling, triangle in the upper left corner, triangle between body and glove, between stick and glove, the goalie's blocking the five-hole, Oak has no intention of going five-hole, seven goals, seven games, seventh grade skating with the varsity on a papal exemption, he brings his blade back, they put him in the *Boston Herald*, they put him in the *Patriot Ledger*, patterns, this is what he told the coaches, the game he scored five goals, the game he scored four, he sees patterns when he sleeps, and later when he doesn't, "Enter Sandman," Shannon in the Boston stands in his varsity jacket as the goalie takes a knee, like the rest of them the goalie plays it safe, goes to BC High, goes to Syracuse, has four kids on Cape Cod, and the goalie's falling, and the rush comes up Oak's feet, leapers in his knees and his legs and his balls and his guts and his lungs and his throat and his face and his brain, backhand, top shelf, red light, board blur, steam from the nose of a giant plastic bull, his teammates on him in a pile, Little Bruins, Bandits, Raptors, Saints, Friars, Griffins, Stars, Bears, Storm.

And when he wakes fully he's sitting on a bench on the bay. He doesn't remember walking there. He's shivering cold. It's 3:00 a.m. He walks the mile back to his mother's house.

39

At 5:00 a.m. he eats the first Dexy. He gets a bellyful of water and whey. He pockets three more and an Oxy 80. If his heart bursts, if his brain bleeds out, it's going to happen on the Worcester ice. He rinses the water glass. His hands bounce around. He holds onto the sink edge and squats. Bursts back up. Drinks some more water. Opens the fridge and Rockys two eggs, throwing the shells into the sink.

Oak goes upstairs to dress. He works himself into the suit he wore for his mother's funeral. He shaves as best as he can around his beard. At the top of the stairs, with his parents' room behind him, he takes a breath. He sees his duffel by the door where he remembered to put it. Oak sees his father sitting in his chair that's no longer there, his ma smoking in hers, Arlene coming back from basketball practice at Our Lady. He shakes off the ghosts. He goes down the stairs, punches the front door frame, gets out into the black cold, and wipes the ice from the windshield of his mother's car. He squats. Thrusts upward. He bends one leg and drops down hard on his groins. Does the other side. He puts his hands on his mother's car and tries to push it over. Everything holds.

Kip is waiting for oak on the avenue when Oak gets there at 6:00 a.m. Kip looks okay, in a jacket and hoodie. When Oak asked Kip if he wanted to ride up to Worcester to watch him play hockey, Kip said sure. Kip gets in. Oak has a plan.

Kellet said he'd have gear for him. Kellet said Oak only has to show up, that Oak can skate on, scrimmage, get a feel for where the Worcester team's at. A thirty-minute bag skate. A thirty-minute scrimmage. The coach, Prieur, is a hard-ass, Kellet said, and slipping Oak into the scrimmage is part of that. Oak's going to beast mode it. He's got a day's dose of Dexy in his pocket. He's going to rail it two hours before the game, stack it with the Oxy. He's got to wake up his legs. After the tryout, he'll go see Barry for more to get him through the season. In the summer, he will get off it all and start the fall healthy and fresh up where he belongs.

Worcester is an hour's drive from Quincy. He wants to get to the rink by ten. He doesn't want to appear too eager, but he wants to get there in time to talk with Kellet, to let Kellet know how he's getting stronger, that he just needs another month to really show what he can still do. Kellet, who he stayed up watching tape with. Kellet, who ran with him in the mornings in Providence when half the guys were cocooned. They'd run down by the Providence River, sometimes puking up the night before. Then they'd run to the Silvertop diner and eat breakfast, drawing scenarios on napkins for upcoming games. Oak knows he's not close to where he's going to be, but he's banking on Kellet remembering what he can do. He'll let Kellet know he's working out, ramping up his ice time. Getting there. He can go for sixty minutes, Oak tells himself. He can go *hard* for thirty minutes. Remind Kellet. Kellet, who he stole a boat with. Let him skate for a month, he's going to say, and he'll be ready to jam by New Year's Day.

"You catch shit?" he asks Kip.

Kip shrugs inside his green hoodie. "Why do you take drugs?"

"To skate."

"They suck."

Oak passes a van.

"You want music?"

"I'm just going to sleep some."

And Kip does, like he hasn't, Kip's hood up over his head, his head against the window. Like how Oak first saw him in the taxi. Kip's out, his breath wheezing, the kid drooling from the corner of his mouth.

AN HOUR LATER Oak pulls into the main entrance to Holy Cross College, fifteen minutes away from the Worcester rink where he's due in two hours. Oak set it up with Arlene who went to Holy Cross to play basketball. She still knows the Holy Cross provost, from when Kyle worked as a student in the provost's office. The provost called the dean of music who Oak talked to on the phone. The dean said there'd be a grad student waiting for them in the college recital hall.

He shakes Kip awake. Kip looks around. "This it?"

"Holy Cross."

Oak parks in the lot outside Fenwick Hall, a columned building with shiny stone steps.

Kip looks at him. "I thought it was gonna be a big-ass rink or something."

"Come on."

They get out of the car. Oak leads Kip up the steps and

through the marble columns. He doesn't tell him anything yet. He doesn't want to spook the kid.

"What are we doing?" Kip says, trying to look cool, trying not to eyeball the whole place and the people in it.

Oak finds the entrance. "Through here." Oak pushes open the big wooden doors.

Arlene told him he wouldn't believe the place and she's right. The recital hall is filled with light, the walls are made of stained glass, the place like a cathedral to music. The ceiling is hung with crystal chandeliers. In the center of the recital hall, on a red oriental rug centered on the polished wood floor, there's a shiny black piano lit by the morning sun.

Oak looks at Kip who is quiet. "You good with it?"

"How do you mean?"

"That piano's for you."

"Nah. Come on."

A black girl, the student, comes in. She smiles at them. "You Tim?"

"Yeah."

"I'm Iris."

"How you doing? This is Kip. He's the musician."

She joins them.

Kip is shaking his head.

"This, Kip, is a Steinway Concert D," Iris says. "There's not many of them. This whole hall is made for sound. Those curtains. Those tiles—"

"You don't have to—" Kips says into the lit, empty space. Kip's face reddens and his eyes well. "I don't want to play here."

The girl looks at Oak.

Kip walks fast back out of the room.

"Give us a minute," Oak says, following Kip.

Outside, Kip is standing in the hallway, small among the hustle of students.

"I don't know her," Kip says when Oak gets there. "You don't have to do this." And then Kip bursts out crying. Like he's eight, and he looks eight, and he turns from Oak to face the wall.

"Hey, Kip."

"I said you don't have to do this."

Oak turns Kip around, Kip's face wet with tears. "You want to play in a catholic school basement your whole fucking life?"

Kip wipes his face with his hoodie sleeve. He doesn't say anything. He walks back into the concert hall. Oak follows him, let's Kip walk ahead alone. Oak sits in the seats by the back wall. Kip stands by the piano in the center of the enormous room, a speck in the light.

"Go for it, Kip," Iris says. She smiles at Kip. She knows enough to walk away.

Kip glances over his shoulder at Oak. Oak shrugs at him, like whatever but inside Oak's rooting for the kid to play. Oak remembers how Shark would put a piece of chocolate in his mouth before he got in the ring. A little caffeine, a little sugar, but mostly a kind of fuck you to the tension of it all. Oak makes a jerk-off motion with his hand at Kip.

Kip sits on the piano bench. He rubs his hands on his pant legs. He pulls the bench in closer to the pedals. Kip tries out a couple keys. Then he starts to play. "Whoa," Kip says, his hands jumping away from the keys.

Iris smiles from the other side of the hall. "Nice, huh?"

Kip brings his fingers down to the keys again. He starts to play. He sits more upright and alert, on the front edge of the piano bench, and Oak sees him transform. Kip's no longer skinny, Kip's no longer a kid. He's a musician. And the sound is something in the hall, with the light coming through the stained glass, with the ebony piano on the red rug. From what Oak hears, and from the look on Iris's face, Kip can play.

Oak gets the Dexy from his pocket. He splits one capsule, shakes the powder into his palm. He splits the second and the third. His heartbeat amps in anticipation of the rush. He's going to pack thirty-six hours into the next three, grind off the edge with the Oxy. Sitting in the back of the recital hall, he leans forward and snorts the speed up his nose.

Oak tries to keep his mind on the ice. He's got an hour and a half. He visualizes himself plumbing the corners, chopping it up in front of the net.

But when Kip moves into a jazzy "White Christmas" and calls out "Ramsey Lewis," Iris starts to sing, and Oak sees his daughter, in the hot rush, standing on the cold beach. Holding the sweater he got her that she didn't want. Kate's full, sweet face, her sunny eyes, crying, the plastic bag blowing from her hand. And the Dexy buckles him and he worries he's going to puke up the whey and the eggs and what's left in his guts of the Oxy. He grips the recital hall bench, his body bursting with sweat. He swallows back the rush, puts his mind in the rink.

"Just like the one I used to know," Kip says to the room.

40

In the car, Kip's looking out the passenger's window. The speed's on Oak fiercely, he's trying to keep it in check until ice time when he wants it to rip.

"I'm sorry I was a pussy," Kip says.

"You did great."

"You think so?"

"Yes. And the girl was impressed too."

Kip stays quiet.

"Your mother ever see you play?" Kip asks.

"Yeah. Yours?"

"No."

Kip reaches into the pocket of his coat. "Here—" It's a burned CD. "Herbie Hancock. You said you liked him."

Kip doesn't look at him.

"Put it on," Oak says.

"Yeah?" Kip slides the CD into the player. "I had to buy a blank CD. It's hard to find. And then I had to use the school computer. So the sound may be whacked."

"You listen to it yet?"

"Just at school. Not at home. I seen you online by the way. Sick."

A piano and then a trumpet and then some serious drums. Oak keeps his focus steady, in his ma's Pontiac, racing toward the Worcester ice.

41

The Worcester Centrum Arena is now the Digital Credit Union Arena. It's a fifteen-thousand-seat rink. Oak skated it once for PC in a special game against Worcester's Clark College. The arena marquee streams a promotion for the upcoming Trans-Siberian Orchestra Christmas Show and then it shows the Worcester Rockets. Oak texts Kellet. Oak shuts down the thought that the guys on the marquee look big and young and strong.

"I never really seen hockey," Kip says. "That time at the rink in Quincy, I never even got to skate."

Oak tells his blasting heart to slow. He's sweated through his dress shirt and pants. He sees himself lying facedown on the Quincy ice, the clock ticking above him, the teenager in the orange safety vest extending his hand.

They stand outside the rink door. Oak punches the metal doorframe.

"Whoa," Kip says.

Oak punches it again, a two-punch. Blood pops from his

knuckles. He grits his teeth, yanks off his shades, stares a death hole into the metal rink door. He opens it.

Rob Kellet is waiting inside. Kellet looks exactly the same—a New Jersey fireplug, the same cropped blond hair, the same scar across his forehead from some high school bender.

"Oak!" Kellet opens his arms, grinning. But as Oak gets closer, Oak sees concern on Kellet's face. They clasp hands and hug.

"You good?" Kellet asks, eying him.

"All good," Oak nods.

"This your kid?"

Kip doesn't say anything.

"Kate's my kid." He's not sure what he's said out loud. "This is my agent," Oak says. Kip smiles.

Kellet leads them past the hand trucks and forklifts, the mixing boards, and the parked Zamboni, along one cement corridor and then another and then into the concourse. They head up steps and into the empty stands and there's the bright, clean ice. Two Rockets skate laps, fast and light.

"You got your pick of seats," Kellet says to Kip.

"I'll sit here," Kip says, pointing at the nearest seat to him. "How will I know which one is you?" Kip says to Oak.

Oak watches the two guys on the ice fly into a blur. He feels his face sliming with thick Oxy sweat, his heart pulsing thickly in his chest.

"He'll be the one badder than the others," Kellet says.

The jumbotron blows a buzzer, then a horn, then clapping hands—the machine running through its paces—and then the numbers on the clock start to whir. Kellet's hand lands on Oak's shoulder. "I'd like to have you back, Oak. Show Prieur what you can do in the corners. He wants to see, you know, *urgency*."

"I was in an accident," Oak says. "All this."

Kellet nods. "I know what you can do, Timmy."

They leave Kip in the stands. Oak follows Kellet down a ramp and through the dressing room tunnel. Kellet pushes open the dressing room door. The familiar smell fills Oak's bones and strengthens him. The guys look up, don't show much. Oak looks over at a tough-looking ginger kid of maybe twenty. The kid glares back.

"This is Tim O'Connor," Kellet announces. Kellet looks out across the team, who nod at him, go about their business. "I'll see you on the ice, Oak," Kellet says.

Oak gets his jacket off. His wet dress shirt. His fist is bleeding. He sits on the dressing room bench, takes off his boots. Takes off his socks. He stands back up, turns to the locker, and checks out the pads they've got him. They won't fit good, but they'll fit good enough.

The Rockets talk low among themselves. About dedication. About playing as a unit. How Prieur is pissed. Slew foot. Five-hole diarrhea. Puck bunnies and hangovers. The cocksuckers in Wilkes-Barre. Oak hears a guy puking loudly in the bathroom stalls. The boys laugh, shake their heads.

Oak pulls his undershirt off.

"Bro," he hears a guy behind him.

Oak turns back, to let them know he'll take it if it's friendly fire, that he'll beat them down a league if it's not. There's more loud puking from the stall, "FUCK ME," and then a stall door swings open and smashes against the wall.

The guys crack up. Oaks laughs too.

A giant comes dragging in from the toilets, his whole face pressed in a towel. He's got a blade scar across his ribs. His shoulders are boulders of bull meat. The giant looks at Oak, his face still hidden in the towel. Something's not right. The guys really start cracking up.

"Fuck me, it's Tim O'Connor—" the giant roars out. "Don't hit me, Oak, I'm already fucked." The guy falls backward toward the wall, pulling the towel from his face to reveal joke store glasses with spring-loaded eyeballs that leap from the sockets and hang there dangling as he falls. "OW, MY EYE!"

The boys look at Oak, for a second the hot locker room air bends and stills, and then they go nuts, the giant coming over, wrapping an arm around Oak's shoulders.

"Gong show, O'Connor," the giant grins, and Oak can smell the guy's puke breath. "We could use a butcher like you." The plastic eyeballs dangle and dance around the giant's mouth. "All these pussies worry about is their hair." The giant goes to get dressed.

Oak goes into the toilet stall. He should be flying with what's in him. Instead, all he's feeling is wrung out. When he gets on the ice, he knows he'll be okay. Once the adrenaline kicks in. When he sees the puck and the young benders in the corner thinking they can jam. He'll be all right. He cracks the last Oxy 80 and sucks it up his nose.

When he gets to the ice, the Rockets are already drilling. The skates Kellet got him are good. He can go sixty on them. The pads don't matter. The sticks Kellet got him are really good. The league is a big step up from Texas. Oak stands at the ramp. His skin hums. His legs, his hip, even his shoulder and spine feel strong and loose. He takes two big breaths. Blows them out. Waits.

At center ice, Kellet stands beside Coach Prieur. The coach is short, bald, and tough-looking. Prieur's got his team skating three-on-two's on a game day.

Oak watches a forward bury the puck, the boys keeping it cool, knowing enough not to celebrate as they skate by, and Oak sees them, and they are that, boys—Canadian major junior league skaters and recent college grads—and then the next line takes off with two guys that can really fly. The winger crashes up the glass in the far corner and then the other wing, 6′ 2″, 220 plus, sandwiches the defender, kicks and snaps the puck out to the blue line, spins away and heads straight at the net, slanting in the shot when it comes.

Kellet and Prieur let the guys have a break after that one, the skaters huddled and laughing. Oak grinds his mouthpiece. He steadies his vision. He can interrupt that. The defenseman needed to control the winger's skates and his legs. The defenseman was too worried about taking an elbow to the face. Oak skates out to center ice. Kellet introduces him to Prieur.

"You'll skate with nine and seven," Prieur says. "Snipers I got, Oak," and he nods at Oak, like he wants Oak to knock the shit out of somebody which he no doubt does, but Oak doesn't know who and he also knows that knocking the shit out of somebody alone isn't going to get him a spot on this team, not with that line, not with the monster puking in the stall. "Good to meet you," Prieur says and the Worcester coach skates down to the other end.

"Okay, Tim," Kellet says.

Kellet splits the team in two. Two lines per side. Oak's on the second line. Oak waits on the Rocket bench. The game is fast, faster than he remembers even Michigan being when he was twenty-two. He's got to grind, in the corners, control it low, remind Kellet how he can get back on defense, how he has always been able to skate both sides of the ice.

The first line comes off, and he's slow to get over the boards, the opposing forward in the white jersey blows right the fuck past him and gets a shot on net. The goalie kicks it out. Oak presses.

There's clear ice behind the net, and Oak swings hard behind it to get some speed, wake himself up, stick-slaps the boards on the fly, wake himself the fuck up, and he and they are flying back up the ice and he sees the emerging pattern, if the two kids he's skating with see what he sees, he's good, and they do and the puck hits his blade across center ice and Oak sets it good on the fly behind him where his defenseman dumps it into the corner and Oak is zoning, the joker giant sweeping behind the net, Oak has a step on the giant and Oak lowers his pain-dead shoulder, keeping the goalmouth in his mind, he's going to ring-up the goon, win the puck, that's what he does, that's what he can do, attack and win. Oak braces for the collision and then all he hits is air and boards. Oak's head bounces off the glass. Oak spins, he's alone in the corner, the puck is nowhere, he stays on his skates, but he doesn't know where he is or where the puck is. Then he comes to and time speeds up fast and the puck is racing away.

Oak rips it to catch up. But it's five on four because of him and the center puts a rope on net, Oak watching his goalie glove it in the air.

Oak's heaving when he gets down to the circle for the face-off.

"You sure you played for Kellet?" a kid with a red beard and a black eye says.

Oak takes it.

His side wins the face-off in their own end. The puck goes behind his net, and his defender wins it and seeing this in a flash Oak is fast back up the boards again, feeling something tearing in his hip, the tear somehow opening and letting him go harder. No one sends him the puck this time down, the puck is on the opposite side of the ice, so Oak sweeps the opponent's net where he knows the puck is going to end up, and he's got big speed, switching zones, and the giant is there again, and this time Oak goes lower and harder and he bundles the goon, Oak hearing it more than feeling it, the goon falling, Oak spinning out toward the net, and the puck is coming, Oak with a leg inside a defender's, a hip inside, he sees the goalie leaning and a flash of the red-bearded kid flying in—and then Oak is in the air, his legs waving like sticks, his head and neck elongating, his arms reaching into nothing. His face slams the ice. His stick slides from him to the boards.

Oak jumps onto all fours like the ice is electric. He shakes his head to feel it. Snot laces out from his nose. He smacks the ice. Gets back up on it. Blows blood from his nose.

The kid with the red beard and the black eye's grinning at him. The kid wants to go. The kid wants to show Coach Prieur his game. And the kid's got game. Oak's still feeling the hit in his bleeding face and his belling head.

"Let's go, Oak," the kid says. The kid knows his name. "I seen you."

Oak skates up to him. Oak can feel the surge building inside. He's going to pop the kid open. He's going to bury that grin in broken teeth. He's got one big shot in him and the kid's going to suffer it. Kellet's holding the puck. The play has stopped. The giant he tipped is standing beside Coach Prier, both men waiting. Kellet is waiting. Around the ice, the Rockets are waiting. Oak sees them, young, hungry, alert, and watching. The kid drops his gloves. Behind him, Oak sees Kip standing in the empty seats.

"Come the fuck on, Pops," the kid says. When the kid drops his helmet, spinning it in a fuck-you, Oak sees the kid's fro of red hair. And he sees Kip sick in the Atomic Burger bathroom, falling against the hand dryer. He sees his daughter crying on the beach.

Oak spits his mouth guard onto the spinning helmet. "Nice

hit," Oak tells him. Oak skates wide around him, leaving the kid with his fists up.

"Yo!" the kid calls after Oak.

"Hey—" Kellet says.

Oak skates past the waiting team, who look at him, unsure. He opens the gate in the boards, steps through, and stands in the ramp between the black concrete walls.

Behind him, he hears a whistle, and the team is skating again.

He looks out at Kip standing alone in the empty stands. Kip doesn't look in his direction. He just stares out at the ice. Oak goes into the locker room. Sees his suit hanging in the locker. He dresses fast. Hangs all the borrowed shit up, wipes the snow off his blades and sets them on the bench. He walks out through the empty DCU arena.

42

Kip's standing at the car. Oak sees he's been crying. Oak opens the car, gets in the driver's side. He jams the key in the ignition. Herbie Hancock comes on.

"You let those guys knock you around." Kip is staring straight out the windshield. Oak stares at the dashboard of his ma's car. What's in Oak, the drugs and the fury, pound at his insides.

"You let those guys walk all over you. You're the pussy. You pussied out. I told you. I told you, you were shit. You're a drug addict. Shit."

Oak feels his own head turning slowly. He looks at the mouthy kid. And then Oak's out the driver's side door. He gets around the car, throws open Kip's door, grabs the kid, pulls him out of the car. Kip falls to all fours. Oak gets his wallet out, takes out a twenty, and throws it at the kid.

"Take the fucking bus."

Oak slams the passenger door, gets around and in. He leaves Kip in the empty Worcester parking lot.

43

Every now and then something streaks by: a red line, an orange line, a yellow light. If the lines hit him, he's dead. Oak knows that. So he rolls on a floor, from his left side onto his back onto his right and back over again. He curls against a wooden bed frame.

He wakes again on his boyhood bedroom floor. His memory is on him now. His face hurts. He rubs a hand across it. On his phone, there's a text from Rob Kellet.

> Oak. What happened, man? Call
> me. We still want you.

Suddenly, Oak remembers waking to find someone trying to machete his throat with a skate. He stands. Looks around. He can't be sure.

44

Chen Seafood is a refrigerated warehouse in Lynn. Inside the office, there's a Chinese guy his age waiting for him. The office is a desk and a computer. Plastic fish on the walls.

He doesn't know what to say. But before he can say anything dumb, like Only sent me, or I'm here to drive the truck, the Chinese guy gets up. "Come with me."

The guy leads Oak back out of the warehouse to where a truck is parked by a fence topped with razor wire. On the other side of the fence is an auto repair yard, with a chained dog sleeping in the cold.

"Okay," the guy says. He hands Oak the keys. It's a step truck. Oak's never had enough shit to haul around, but it looks like a U-Haul rental, a square box with a regular dash and no stick. He can drive it. He can get it down 93 to 95 to Providence. But first he's got to get it down Route 1. Route 1 with the stores and the lights and the places to get pulled over.

"What's in it?" he asks the guy.

The guy's wiry, serious.

"Seafood."

"Show me."

The guy looks at him. Goes to the back of the truck and opens it.

Inside, there's six refrigerated metal tanks strapped to the bay walls, each the size of a locker.

The guy steps up into the truck, unlatches the nearest tank. Lifts the lid. Oak steps forward to see.

Inside the tank is a swirling mass of live eels.

The guy closes the lid. Steps toward the edge of the truck.

"Okay?"

"And the others?" Oak says.

"Same."

Oak steps up into the truck, points at one in the back. "Show me that one."

The guy walks between the tanks to the back, unlatches the tank, opens it. Eels.

"Seafood."

Oak nods.

The guy gets out of the truck without saying anything more.

THERE'S NO RADIO IN THE CAB, just his thoughts and the metal tanks scraping the metal truck floor. Oak gets the truck onto Route 1. He's blinking sweat out of his eyes. He hears the metal tanks, jumping with every pothole. He's called Slats five times. He sees Slats running from the building site in the night. There's a red light up ahead. Oak stops the truck three feet behind a white van.

The white van's windows are tinted. He sees the sky and other cars reflected. He keeps his eyes forward. He's wearing a Friars hat he found in his closet. He gives his face a quick wipe with his sleeve. He doesn't like the van's tinted windows. He doesn't know who's looking at him. It could be cops, it could be guys getting ready to roll him, to steal whatever is in with the eels.

He opens the glove compartment. It's empty. He looks down into the passenger door pocket that's stuffed with paper. He pulls the papers away. There's a leather satchel jammed under the papers. Oak stares at it. The sunlight beats on his eyes. He picks up the satchel and puts it on his lap. It's heavy. The light goes green. He opens the satchel as the white van pulls ahead. The gun is black and oily. Colt Automatic Caliber .25 is etched on the barrel, a rearing horse on the grip. The sun flashes against the windshield, and the white van is gone.

45

Oak finds Basco and Sons, a windowless metal warehouse, down the hill from Schneider Rink where his number's on a plaque in the PC Friartown hall of fame. There's nobody there. The fence around the warehouse is padlocked.

Drugs. Money. A body cut in pieces. He shakes that off. He's early. He doesn't want to sit in the truck outside the building. He drives up the hill and pulls over on the always empty streets behind the PC arena. He gets out of the truck. He unlocks and rolls up the truck bay door. He gets inside the back of the truck and lowers the door into darkness.

Inside, Oak waits for his eyes to adjust. He hears his own blood pulsing inside his ears. He hears the soft hiss of the motors that keep the eels cold and breathing. He goes to the first of the tanks that the Chinese guy didn't open. Oak draws in a slow, tight breath. He lifts the lid.

Eels. Water. Ice. He slams the lid shut.

He moves to the next tank. Opens it. The same.

The next. Same. Nothing but water, ice, and eels.

Oak knows the last tank has something in it. When he gets closer, he sees the last tank has blood on the latch. It's a fish truck, he tells himself. There's fish blood. Blood on the wooden fish priest in a boat. Him and Major and a chest of empty beer. He's telling himself. Fish bleed. He's telling the parts of him that are telling him to run. To drive the truck back to Lynn. To leave it behind the PC rink and go.

In this last tank, he tells himself, there are going to be eels. He reaches for the bloody latch.

There's a rap on the closed truck door.

Oak stands still in the darkness. The gun is in the glove box where he stashed it. His fists buzz, hanging at his sides. He hears again the blood inside his ears.

It comes again, the rapping, the sound bouncing against the dark metal walls. He knows it's a cop. He knows it's real.

Oak wipes his face on his sleeve. "Just a second."

He lifts the truck door into a swirl of police lights.

"You don't look Chinese," the cop says. "Everything all right here?"

Oak sees that the cop is just a Providence College cop, not a real one. Oak gets down fast beside him.

"One of my crates got loose."

"You got paperwork?"

"And I used to skate over there. I'm early on a delivery. Tim O'Connor. I thought I might check out the ice, like a geezer."

"Can I get a look in those crates?" the cop says.

The cop's probably run the plates already. Oak figures he'd be in cuffs if the plates weren't okay.

"Yeah. No problem."

Oak gets back up into the truck, opens one of the front tanks fast, to keep the cop on the road, to show him the eels.

"Jesus," the cop says.

"Yeah—"

"Who the fuck eats those things?"

"Chinese, I guess. I'm just the Sunday driver. Pocket money."

Oak opens the other front crate fast, like he's going to open them all if the cop wants.

"I got it," the PC cop says, shaking his head.

Oak gets back down to the road, rolls the truck door shut behind him.

"You used to skate?" the PC cop says.

The cop's looking at him like he's a sorry bastard, driving a truck under the table for the Chinese.

"Class of '07."

"You beat up on Brown?"

"You know we did."

The PC cop nods. "Take care of yourself, guy."

"You too."

The PC cop pulls away.

Oak stands in the bright sun. When he is sure the cop is gone, he gets back up into the truck. He gets his hands on the bloody latch of the last tank. With a fast inhale he opens the tank lid.

Oak stares at a mass of swirling eels. They don't need him to drive eels. They don't need him to be Mr. Chen, to get paid in cash, by Georgians, who Slats knows, who run a copper scam for idiots. Like Slats. Like him. Oak rolls up his sleeve. He makes a fist. He has to know. He raises his fist above the writhing ball of eels. On an in-breath he plunges his fist down into the water. Eels squeeze out from beneath his knuckles. His fist finds the bottom of the tank. He drags his fingers slowly through the icy water, the eels thick and slow around his skin. There's nothing in there. He yanks his arm out of the freezing water. Sucks in air. He slams the tank lid and latches it.

Oak moves back to the next tank. Opens it. His hand is still in a hard fist. He jams down into the eels and water. They look like black snakes.

Nothing. He yanks his arm out.

He goes to the next tank. Nothing. By the last tank Oak wants to punch every eel between their ice-cold eyes.

He drives down the hill to Basco and Sons. The gate's open. Oak parks the truck by the icy, wet loading dock. The gun's in the glove compartment. He takes it out. Looks around. Puts it back. He's buzzing. He goes around the front of the warehouse to the entrance.

Inside, there's a small office, with fish on the walls, a map of Italy, a PawSox calendar and a Friars banner, with an old guy in a sweater eating a sandwich.

The old guy looks up. "You the Chen guy?"

Oak nods.

"I'll meet you around the back."

Oak goes outside, waits by his truck. The loading dock is separated from the warehouse by heavy plastic strips. He sees guys in waders working big trays of ice and fish. He can hear Spanish and a radio.

The old guy pushes through the strips out onto the bay with two guys in aprons and waders, one of them with an orange knit hat over dreads.

The guys don't look at him. They get into the bay and haul the tanks away. The old guy's still eating his sandwich. One, two, three, four, five, six. Whatever is in the tanks is gone. The old guy looks down at Oak.

"You want something for the road?" the old guy says. "My wife makes them."

"What was in those tanks?" he says it steady.

The old guy shrugs, olive oil leaking down his hand. "Capitone. Eels." He nods at Oak, Oak standing there, the guy going back through the stained plastic refrigeration strips, yelling something in Spanish.

HE'S DRIVING I-95. The back of the truck is silent now. The air in the cab is silent. He's seeing Slats running. Slats taking Kate's hand. What Only told him. What Kip said. He's seeing the black knots of eels. His knuckles are bleeding. The scar tissue on his right middle and ring fingers has torn away. He sees his knuckles bleeding on the wheel.

The metal road dividers blur. And he gets it, all at once. The eels were in mesh baskets. The mesh scraped the skin from his knuckles. Basco or whatever the fuck his name is will lift the mesh baskets from the tanks, throw the eels in a fucking dumpster, and, below, in the black water, the real delivery will be vacuum sealed.

Back at Chen's Seafood, Oak sits in the cab of the truck. They're not going to shoot him. He's not going to shoot them.

The Chinese guy comes out of his office and walks across the small, empty lot.

He'll never know. Drugs. Money. Saba told him where the gun would be.

The Chinese guy is walking straight at him. Expressionless. There's nobody around but the dog turning circles on its chain.

Oak snaps open the glove compartment. He grabs the gun. Oak shoves the gun into his jacket pocket. Shuts the glove compartment. Checks his face in the rearview mirror. The gun sits in his pocket like a puck. The guy rolls up the door.

Oak steps out.

"You get paid from your boss," the Chinese guy says, rolling the truck door down and locking it. Behind the Chinese guy, another Chinese guy, older, comes out of the office and stands there, at a distance, watching. The guy lights a cigarette.

Oak doesn't know if they know about the gun. He doesn't know if they work for Only. In his head, he sees Slats on the phone, he sees Slats making calls, he sees Slats with Kate laughing with the Georgians and the Chinese while Oak gets his head kicked in behind the warehouse.

"Okay," the younger Chinese guy says, nodding, walking past Oak to get up into the driver's seat of the truck.

Oak watches the guy get into the driver's seat. He can say he forgot he took the gun. Give it back straight. But the guy starts the truck without checking the glove compartment. The older guy goes back inside the office. Oak walks at an angle to his ma's car, keeping an eye on the Chinese guy, keeping an eye on Slats in his head.

46

He hauls back down Route 1. He's hauling adrenaline inside his blood, trying to breathe it back, to keep his mind in the car. He's calling Slats. Six times in a row. Slats is not answering because he set Oak up, left him on the roof to hang. Oak sees Esteban in the hospital in his metal crown. The sun flashes the windscreen. Oak closes his eyes. He's driving. He opens them. The ramp to Southie, past the food bank, is in the lane to his right. He veers the car over, some guy honking, and rolls it down the ramp. He's trying to slow his heart and head. The backs of his eyes are pounding. A car swings by close. Another. He speeds down Broadway.

Oak finds Slats in the Christmas tree lot in front of the Liquor Mart. Slats is running a spruce through a netting barrel for a mother and her kid. Oak jumps out of the car, the car door open and beeping. A Salvation Army Santa is ringing a bell. Above him, the Liquor Mart sign buzzes as it spins.

"Whoa, Oak," Slats says when he gets there. Slats tries to smile.

"No weed in these trees?" Oak says to Slats, steady.

"Not that I know of," Slats says, making a nervous joke, but Oak is not joking, he's not there to make jokes with what Slats has done. "You left your car door open, man."

"I want to talk to you."

"I'm working here."

Oak puts his arm on Slats's skinny shoulders, moves them away from the customers and trees. "I've been calling you."

"I've been in Vermont. No service." Slats shakes his head. "What's going on, Oak? You're sweating like a motherfucker. Your hands are bleeding."

Behind Slats, a couple of little kids jump around a tree that their father hoists toward their car.

"Shannon says you saw Kate." Slats shakes his head, but Oak sees the fear in his eyes. "She couldn't sleep. We found her standing on the street in front of our house, Oak, crying. At like four in the morning. Shannon has to be at work, can't go back to sleep. It's not, Kate's not always as stable as she appears, let's leave it at that. She's been doing good. I want her to continue to do good. It's Christmas for fuck's sake, Oak."

Santa's laughing with his bell.

"You set me up, Kevin?" Oak tries to keep his voice steady. When Oak steps forward he feels the weight of the gun in his coat pocket.

"What?" And the way Slats smiles again, the way Slats's eyes go wider, the whole face Slats makes without knowing he's making it, gives Slats away.

Oak grabs the collar of Slats's jacket. Oak brings his face close. "Did you set me up, Kevin?" Oak squeezes the collar, Slats's jacket bunching in his fists. "Answer me."

"Jesus, Oak—"

"I saw you running."

"Get the fuck off me." Slats shoves him off. "You're fucked up." Slats walks quickly past Oak, back toward the stand of trees, back toward the safe cluster of shoppers.

"You don't want me near her."

People turn to look at Oak.

"Fuck off."

"Hey," Oak hears a father say in a blur. Oak rushes Slats. He gets his arms hard around Slats's waist and drives Slats backward off his feet and into a standing group of roped-together Christmas trees. The trees topple as one beneath them, Oak on Slats, crashing down onto the falling trees, a sharp green branch slicing Slats's forehead when they hit the blacktop.

Oak's face is inches from Slats's. "You don't want me near her? So you throw me to the cops?"

"You come home, for your mother, you come back," spit from Slats's bleeding face sprays at Oak, "you're all fucked up. *Where's my daughter? Where's my daughter? Your* daughter? Fuck you, Oak. Fuck you." Slats tries to get out from under him, smacks at Oak's face with his pinned arm. "You weren't fucking there. You aren't fucking *here*."

Oak pulls the gun fast, presses it to Slats's head. They're so close, no one can see it but them. "You set me up."

"I only wanted it to scare you. I knew you'd get away . . ." Slats goes quiet. He looks at the gun. He looks at Oak. "Go ahead," Slats says, a whisper, Oak's hand on his neck, the gun on Slats's cheek. "Show her."

Oak looks at the gun in his hand. At the dent of flesh in his friend's face. All of his focus is there: black metal on white skin, the gun barrel shaking in his hand.

He pushes off Slats. He shoves up to his feet, stuffing the gun back into his jacket. There's a crowd around them, a whirl of parents and kids. Oak walks across the liquor store parking lot. The car door is open. He leaves Slats lying in the trees.

47

Barry said to meet him at a bar on Broadway, to sit at a table and wait. The place is new, high-end. Oak gets himself to a table at happy hour, waits on his uncle. He orders a beer. A woman comes in and walks up to him, carrying a plastic Nike Store bag. She joins him before he recognizes her. It's Barry's girlfriend.

"Barry can't make it," she says.

She puts the Nike bag on the table. She pulls out a shoe box.

"Here are the shoes." She makes a kind of show of opening the box, like he's been waiting on the shoes. She removes the tissue paper from around the shoes and there's a nice pair of Nike Air. She wraps them back up, closes the lid, and puts them back in the bag.

"Barry says you should stay and eat," she says. "I gotta go."

Barry's girlfriend takes off, leaving Oak with the heroin-stuffed shoes.

The waitress comes over.

"It's just me, I guess," Oak says.

48

The streetlight falls on the poster of Ray Borque that's lying on his bedroom floor. The yellow blanket slants off the curtain rod, the curtains hang torn from their broken hooks. The streetlight illuminates Borque, smiling up at Oak. Inside that smile, Oak sees something, in the dark behind Borque's teeth. Something like the black gun there in his hand, a black hole, black into black, the pistol metal warm now and slick, Oak's eyes going from it to the curtains, to the torn posters and trophies and broken glass on his bedroom floor. The engraving on the pistol grip reads: Made in Hartford on May 28, 2007. The year he graduated from PC.

He points the gun at the yellow blanket. He points the gun at the poster of Ray Borque lying on the floor. He points it at the mirror where he sees himself reflected. He bends his elbow and points the gun barrel between his own eyes. Sees the look in Slats's eyes. Sees his daughter on the beach. Squinting, he can walk down that black tunnel, into a still place. His phone rings.

Three a.m. It's Joan.

"Hey?"

He's dreaming.

"How is he?" she asks.

"He's all right."

"I was wondering."

Oak sits on his bed with the gun in his hand.

"You took Charlie's pills?"

"Yes."

Oak hears Joan exhale. He imagines her smoking and shivering in her cold yard.

"Where are you, Joan?"

"I'm sorry, Tim." Her voice comes in gasps. "To call you like this."

"Will you go inside the house? Are you outside?"

"Sure, Tim."

He doesn't know who to call. He gets into his ma's car. He drives it straight, down along Broadway and onto Dot Ave. He drives past where he decked the cop. He drives past Donahue's bar. He drives the route he rode his bike on as a boy, toward the expressway and Shark's red-painted cinder block gym.

She's at her door as he comes up her walkway. She lets him in. She stands in the foyer. She hasn't touched anything in the dining room, hasn't put the lids back on the paint cans. The cans are sitting there, drying out among the newspapers and tarps. The ladder still leans on the wall.

She's standing there, the light from the kitchen putting her in shadow. She looks too scared. It's luck that he doesn't fall. He takes the pain in his back and drives it into the ground through his heels, pours it out in sweat.

"You okay?"

"I washed your shirt. From last week."

He sees Slats's blood on the one he's still wearing. Joan steps closer. He reaches out for her and she is inside of his arms. He feels her heart beating, quick against him.

Her hands run over his skin inside the jersey. He feels embarrassed, suddenly, for his skin, for his knuckleless hands, for his fake tooth, for his busted-flat nose. He keeps his eyes on hers. He feels the warmth of her and he remembers them dancing and he wants that warmth, his hands feeling dumb on her skin, her lips floating, he feels her breath, and he kisses her.

She lifts his jersey, Oak's teeth clenching, and she takes off her turtleneck, and they move to the sofa, taking off his sweats and her jeans, her breath bursting from her, then his, she kisses him hard, and she's there and she isn't, her eyes staring past him when they open but her arms are tight around his back, he tries to keep his weight off her, and she's moving with him, and he's tumbling, and she is, he feels it, they are together in a place he knows they won't go again, and Joan rises up and moves him so that she is across him and he watches her above him and then a flash, Joan's eyes look down into his, and it's not fear in her that he sees but something larger, that which is behind fear, and Oak brings her to him when they finish, to press that emptiness away.

He slides from her to the floor. He rests his face on the sofa cushion. They breathe together. Her eyes are shut. Her face is to the ceiling. Oak brings his fingers to her cheek, kisses her there, her damp hair to his lips.

"Being with Charles," she says it to the ceiling, like it is what they've been talking about, "it became like living with a brother. A brother I really loved. He was the most beautiful man."

He smooths her hair from her forehead.

"He died of stomach cancer. We were signed up to do a biath-lon. Because I can't really swim."

Oak gets himself up on the sofa. He curls her to him, their bodies warm with sweat. He holds her inside his arms. She wraps his hand in hers. He feels her quick breath. He holds her there. He'll hold her until morning. He'll hold her until Christmas and New Year's Day, until the snow melts and the beech leaves open. And then she is twitching, and she is gone.

HE HEARS BIRDSONG. With her breathing.

***

Later, there's a dog barking, and the sound of a truck in the driveway.

"It's the milkman," Joan says, her voice startling him. Her back is still against him. They haven't moved.

"You have a milkman?"

"They make the best chocolate milk."

She turns to face him. She smiles, too quick. He kisses her. She kisses him back, but only for a second. She pulls back the blanket he put across them in the night. His blood's on it. There's some on her skin. And under her hazel eyes, dark circles, like she hasn't slept when he knows that she has.

"I have to get on the floor—" he says.

"It's all right, Tim."

He can't even make it to find his shorts. He drops onto her floor, naked.

She leaves him there.

WHEN HE GOES TO THE KITCHEN in his pants and shirt, she's in a robe and he can see that she's been crying.

"We've got a trial date," she says. "Two months. I was going to tell you yesterday."

"Okay, Joan."

"The Assistant DA is giving us two weeks to settle."

He nods slowly at her.

"He doesn't mean it, he'll settle to the end, they'll make him. He just wants the case done with, Tim. More than before. We can bargain with that. A year, maybe. That means six months at Plymouth. I'm still pressing for treatment court. And if we go to trial, we could fly your Coach Tom Bowie up, as a character witness. Maybe even Cpt. MacIvoy. Jim Sharkey. You got friends, Tim—"

"Hey," he says, to stop her.

She looks at him. Nods quickly.

He goes out to the front porch. Snow covers the grass and sparkles in the sun. He gets the chocolate milk that's in a small metal tray. Brings it in. Gets the lid off the milk and pours it in a pot.

"You got eggs in this joint?"

She shakes her head.

"Bread?"

She nods, smiles a little. "Yes."

He puts some bread in the toaster. He stirs the heating milk to have something to do.

"We can't . . . It'd never work, Tim. I'm sorry."

"Yeah."

"I'm sorry."

He puts the toast on the table in front of her.

"I'll find you a good lawyer," she says. She heads from the kitchen, away down the hall.

When she doesn't come out, he goes down the hallway, past the husband's room. In the shadows of the hallway, he sees her sitting at the bar at Donahue's, feels her cold in his arms on the dance floor, hears her voice on the phone in the night. Standing alone in her backyard. Nodding off at her desk.

The bathroom door is open. He goes in. She is sitting on the toilet, on the closed seat, staring into nothing.

"I was wondering," she says, not looking at him.

There's no needle, there's no syringe. Just a small glass tube, a hand mirror, and a pill box filled with heroin.

"Here, Tim."

She holds the pill box out to him, the mirror.

"I can't do it, with my hands how they are," Oak says.

Joan nods. She shakes some of the heroin onto the mirror for him. She uses the straw to draw a rough line.

He kneels beside her by the toilet. He takes the glass straw. The end of the straw dances around the bottom of the rail and then he sucks in hard, drawing the fire up into his nose and deep inside his blood.

He waits. He feels it happening fast. He doesn't collapse to the tiles. He crawls and sits himself carefully against her coral blue tub. He doesn't feel sick and then he wonders why he would feel sick and then he remembers he did a line of heroin. He had a summer job on the ferries to the Harbor Islands. He thought sometimes he would like to build boats. There was a place in Maine. Wooden boats. He sees the sun fall on cove-protected dories, their hulls white and green and red. Joan is taking her robe off and is running the bath. She gets in it, and he's watching her, her skin and the water mixing.

"I'm warm," he says, and she smiles and he wants that smile, to be near it, and they are warm and liquid together, heat around them in waves.

And then he is in the bath with her, and the shower curtain has fallen around them, he thought it was a blue sail, and there's blood in the bath water and she is sitting between his opened legs.

HE WAKES TO SOMETHING JUMPING against his chest and legs. It's Joan. They're in the bath. She's shivering. He sees one of his stitches floating in the water.

"Joan?"

She shifts in his arms. He doesn't know how long he has been there. The water's cold and the air is cold. He grabs the tub edge and lifts them to sitting. She lies back in the cold water as he steps out of the tub.

"Wake up." He lifts her to standing. The bathwater sheets from her skin. She falls a little toward him as she steps out of the tub. "Come on," he says, wrapping her in her robe.

He gets them to the sofa, her feet slipping on the kitchen floor. He can't carry her up the stairs.

"I'm good," she says. He gets the blanket over her. He feels his body drop to the floor against the sofa.

When he wakes again, from a dreamless, dead place, she's gone. He goes up the stairs to find her sleeping in her bed. He watches her breath rise and fall.

He goes back down the stairs. In the bathroom, he looks at the pill box, the straw, and the mirror. He thinks about the shit Barry gave him. About the gun on his dresser. He hangs her shower curtain back up. He lets the bathwater down the drain.

49

Later, Oak sits in his mother's kitchen. The snow's coming down now. He called Joan twice and texted her, but she hasn't called or texted back. He watches the snow out the window in the street-light. He feels her in his arms. He sees her eyes. He looks at the two small baggies of heroin that Barry pressed into his hand. They're in a bowl on the table with car keys and house keys and loose change. He felt warm inside of his bones with her in her bath, before the shower curtain fell and they woke shivering and numb. He understands now in part why she's seemed so dreamy. The night before with her phone call and the gun, it was like a dream leading to a dream leading to a dream. She won't want to see him again. He understands how she might just have needed to be with someone to help her push away the past, however briefly. Even him.

He picks up a baggie. It fits in the center of his palm. He knows it's poison. It felt like poison when it was inside him. It won't help his body. It won't help his game. But he's wondering if he even has game anymore. If he even has any kind of body that is worth helping. He feels the slight weight of the small bag, brushes his thumb across it. A whole world in a square inch. Snow blows against the window. His ma hated snow. Her grave is getting pasted. He tosses the heroin back into the bowl. He stares into it. The contents of the bowl zoning.

Someone pounds on the front door. Oak's hands jump on the table.

It's Only with a gun, he thinks. Or Barry with more drugs for him to sell. Or maybe something that lives only inside of his head.

The doorbell rings. And rings again. Then the house goes quiet. Oak gets up from the kitchen table, walks into the front hallway. He opens the front door. "Hola," he says.

He feels the cold first. A rush that freezes his insides instantly, that makes him solid ice.

Kip is standing on the front steps streaked in blood. His hair. His face. A bleeding ghost. It's a vision from hell, Oak knows it, it's not real, it's his punishment, this visitation, it won't go, he'll live with it, following him when he works and when he sleeps. Oak shakes his head against it, but it is still there.

And then time explodes and Oak is burning hot, leaping toward the boy, gathering Kip in, Kip's blood on Oak's hands and face. The foyer spins. Oak sucks air, trying to warm the kid with his grip. He thinks to feel Kip's head. Gets a finger in a gap where the blood still flows, thick, in Kip's hair. Oak presses against the gap. Kip keeps shaking. He holds Kip in front of him and lifts the boy's hoodie and shirt. When he sees Kip's torso he can only fold forward, to press his forehead against Kip's, to hold the boy by his skinny shoulders that drip down along his battered and bleeding skin.

50

The ambulance took forever. They hurried Kip onto a stretcher and drove him away, Oak following in his mother's car, watching Kip get wheeled into the emergency room. They took Oak's statement.

Oak didn't give up Kip's old man. Not yet.

Oak's at Kip's house in Quincy before he even realizes he's been driving again.

Oak gets out of the car and walks to Kip's front door. The front door is ajar.

Inside, the house is shadowy. Oak finds a light switch and hits it: the living room is in chaos. Hundreds of record albums are broken, bent and scattered across the floor. The shelves that held them are smashed and ripped from the walls. A stereo is hammered into pieces. The gold hammer that Oak bought Kip rests in the middle of it all.

Oak walks across the room and picks the hammer up.

He goes up the stairs.

To make him eat it.

At the top of the stairs, Oak hurls open the first door that he sees. It's Kip's room. There's a poster of Miles Davis. There's blood on the bed.

Oak steps back into the hall. He feels calm, the familiar feeling of the lightness inside the blackness of impending violence. He walks down the hall. There's a light ahead of him from a partially opened door. Oak gets his hand on the father's doorknob. He lifts the hammer high. "You gonna shoot me, Papi?" Oak says. He kicks open the door. "You gonna shoot me after what you did to your own son?"

Kip's father lies motionless in his bed, in the lamp light.

Oak squeezes the hammer in his hand, feels the weight of it. He walks inside the warm adrenal hum to the side of Kip's father's bed. Oak raises the hammer above the guy's forehead. Kip's father doesn't move.

Oak swings the hammer down and smashes the mattress inches from the guy's head. Kip's father doesn't flinch. Oak sees the blood on the guy's hands and face.

Oak raises the hammer again. "He's your son," Oak says, the hammer shaking in his own hand. "He's your own fucking son."

The guy's face is right there, flat, dumb, dead but alive. The weight of the hammer will smash in his skull, shatter his teeth, drive his nose backward into his brain. Oak brings the hammer high, to finish the guy. The guy looks like Kip. Oak sees Kip on the stretcher. He sees McDonald's bleeding eye. Oak turns from Kip's father's face and hurls the hammer across the room. The hammer bounces off a wall and spins to the floor. Oak grabs the table lamp, and then Oak finds the lamp in his hand, and he is standing at the top of the stairs. He hurls the lamp, the glass shattering before him in the foyer. Oak walks down the stairs through the shattered glass and back out into the street.

51

Oak sits in the hospital garage, waiting on morning. He can't stop shaking.

In the morning, he tells the nurse at the desk that he's a family friend.

"The little boy that was all beat up?" another nurse, a black nurse, says to the white nurse.

"I'm the one who brought him in last night," Oak says.

"His father's in there with him right now." The black nurse shakes her head. "I don't know what happened . . ."

"There's no mother," the white nurse says.

"That's for sure."

"His father?"

The white nurse picks up the phone.

"What are you doing?"

"I'm going to see if it's okay that you go in."

"What room is he in?"

She holds up her finger, one minute.

"Go on in," the black nurse says. "Two-eighteen, down the hall."

Oak can't believe the guy fucking showed. He's not certain what's going to happen when he gets in the room with him. He breathes against a surging fury.

In the room, Kip's father is holding Kip's hand and crying through swollen eyes. "I called every hospital," Kip's father says.

When Oak looks at Kip, he has to take two breaths, to keep his heart alive.

"She got a sister," Kip's father says, stroking Kip's hand, not taking his eyes from his son. "She always wanted him to come live with her. Got a couple other kids. Out in Springfield."

Kip's eyes are shut. He's got saline stuck in him. Oak knows what he looks like under the sheet. Kip's hair is cut. A patch of his scalp is stitched. His right ear is bandaged. There's a red welt horizontally across his chin.

"He's resting," Kip's father says. The guy's in some kind of heavy shock. "My heart's dry from crying."

Oak steps toward the bed. Kip's father doesn't move. Oak's not even sure if the guy registers who he is. Oak gently lifts the sheet to see. Kip's ribs are bandaged, his skin is red and black now with bruises. Oak lowers the sheet. He presses his forehead to Kip's busted face. Kip opens his swollen eyes.

"Oak," Kip says, spaced out. "You were scoring, dude. And I was playing piano in the stands."

Kip's eyes close again.

Oak leans back up. "What's her name?"

Kip's father does not respond.

"What is the name of your wife's sister?" He says it steady, shoving the rage down into his legs and through the cold white hospital floor.

"Pia."

"Call her."

"I don't got her number."

"What's her last name?"

Kip's father thinks for a long time. "Martinez."

"And the husband?"

"Paul."

Oak gets out his phone. They're listed.

The sister-in-law answers.

"Pia," Oak says, "I am a friend of Kip's." Oak realizes he doesn't even know Kip's last name.

"Kip?"

"His father is going to jail."

"Who is this?"

She calls out to her husband.

The guy gets on. *"¿Qué paso?"*

"Paul, yo soy un amigo de Kip. Habla Ingles?"

"Kip? Si?"

"His father beat the shit out of him. Will you and your wife take Kip? He says you'll take Kip."

There's silence.

"Paul?"

"I know this is true," Paul says.

"Si, ahora estoy en el hospital," Oak says.

"Tu eres el doctor?"

"Here." Oak hands the phone to Kip's father.

"Hola, Paco," Kip's father says, slumping over his son, not letting go of Kip's hand.

Oak gets out of that room. He heads hard down the corridor, the corridor bucking until he has to lean against a wall. The white nurse at reception looks at him. It's like she's swimming.

"You all right?"

"Where's the other nurse?"

"I don't know—"

"Get her."

"Sir, I—"

"I said fucking get her."

He closes his eyes. Time passes.

"You wanted to see me?" The black nurse is there with a security guard, standing with the white nurse behind the desk.

He looks at her. "Kip's father is the one who did him in. He's in there now. The guy that did him."

And then he sort of falls forward, and then the two nurses and the security guard are walking him to a chair, and he's sat there, waiting on the police, they got him water, and a towel, watching the scene like he's been hit in the head, like it's happening on TV, the voices in static, the picture in snow.

52

His head is being kicked from every direction, his brain ringing inside the busted roaring of his beaten scalp. With every shot a picture: *ping*, and there's Kip on all fours in the Worcester parking lot; *ping*, there's Joan in the bathtub, naked in his arms; *ping*, there's his ma, smoking on the beach; *ping*, there's his boyhood dog Johnny, Johnny the bitch!; *ping*, there's his daughter in his arms no bigger than his head. "Get me out of here," he's yelling. He's pulled out. He's lying in a tray of his own sweat. He shakes off the nurse's hand and sits up to see a doctor.

"From now on, Mr. O'Connor," the doctor says, "you are going to have to take very, very good care of yourself, okay?"

53

Oak gets out of the car and stands in front of Shark's gym, his breath bursting from him. The lights are on. Oak lets himself in. He goes into Shark's office to shut the lights off, but Shark is in there sitting at his desk, staring at the photos on his wall.

"Oh. Tim." Shark's lips waver after he says Oak's name. "It's bullshit, Oak." Shark removes his big glasses. Shark wipes his face. "I guess maybe I was waiting for you to show. I guess maybe that's why I'm still here."

Oak stands in the office doorway.

"When you came in for the haircut, I knew right away what it was about."

Oak nods.

"My Angie," Shark shakes his head. Shark reaches for a manila envelope. He shakes the contents onto the desk: photographs, postcards, what looks like a report card from school. "That's all I got, Tim." Shark stares into the pile in his lap. "I thought maybe when Marlene died . . . but nothing. Not a word."

Shark picks out a postcard, holds it in his big, marbled hands.

Greetings from California: oranges, the Hollywood sign, the Golden Gate Bridge.

"I looked on the internet. Called up a boy she used to see in school. Called the police. Called the social services . . ."

The office lights hum overhead. Water bangs in the pipes. Thirteen, fourteen, fifteen. The serenity prayer.

"Let's fight," Oak says.

Shark looks up from the postcard, like Oak's not there, like Shark's heard a ghost.

"I'll hold the pads," Oak says, and he wants it, to be in the ring, to pound out what's in him, to watch Shark move and slide and be young again. "See what you got."

"What I got is old," Shark says. But Shark nods, nods a little more. "You have your tryout?"

"It didn't go so good." Oak feels himself shaking again, like in the garage. He crosses his arms in front of his body. He feels himself falling again but he knows he's standing and he presses all of his weight down into the concrete floor.

Shark's staring at him. "Let me get some liniment." Shark gets up from his desk. Shark takes off his buttoned shirt, puts on a sweatshirt. Shark's still in his brown slacks as they get up into the ring. Oak puts on the pads. Shark rubs his special-blend liniment over his hands and elbows and shoulders. He slips on goggles. The top of Shark's head is already beading sweat at his hairline.

"Nothing fancy," Shark says, and he puts on his gloves. Oak starts to move. Shark straight-punches a left. The weight of Shark's punch passes through the pad and out the back of Oak's hand. Shark throws an even harder right, the pad popping, the punch ringing Oak's head. *Choices.* Punch to the body. *Choices.* Uppercut to the chin. *Choices.* Hook, bolo, jab. Legs or biceps? School or the street? *Choices*. Shark strikes with the left, almost quicker than Oak can catch, and now Shark's punches wave in, pop, pop, pop, Shark's eyes burning and relaxed, killing and saving, and then Shark lands a right hook that they both know would drop a bull and Shark's name bursts from Oak's lips, Oak spinning with the force to save his shoulder.

"Damn!" Shark laughs, admiring his own punch. "I need to sit *down*!"

Shark leans on the top rope, breathing. His sweat rolls down his face, his sweatshirt wet from it. Oak wraps an arm around Shark's shoulders and presses his own dripping forehead to Shark's wet cheek and they lean there together, looking out across the dark, empty gym.

"Thanks, buddy," Shark says, like Oak's the one holding him up.

54

When Shannon comes into the Broadway Diner, Oak sees again how much Kate looks like her. She joins him at the counter, but she doesn't sit down.

Shannon stands there in her coat and scarf, looking at him like she might not stay.

"I got us pie," he says. They ate it back when they came to the diner to do homework.

The guy behind the counter puts the pie down. Oak doesn't want it, but he wants her to have it, so he gets a fork into his slice.

"You're shaking." She says it quietly.

He pushes the pie around on the plate with the fork.

"It took me an hour to get here," Shannon says.

When he called her, he could tell Slats hadn't told her about the Christmas trees or the gun. He wasn't going to deny it if Slats had. He's looking at the pie. He's only hearing his own breath. His throat is shutting down, his breath rasps inside him. He wants to tell her about Kip but there isn't any point to it. He's been apart from her too long.

"You said you wanted to talk about Kate."

"Is Kevin a good father?"

When she doesn't respond, he looks up.

"Kevin?" she says. "Yes."

Oak nods. He feels tears coming out of his eyes, and it's ugly, sitting there at the diner counter, with tears again in his beard. "I want to try to see her again."

"Kate's fourteen, Tim. Kevin's out in the snow selling trees. I work for two asshole doctors so we can have insurance. I put on nice clothes and get up every morning to make sure Kate gets to school because some nights she spends the whole time being scared. Of nothing real. Just raw fear." Shannon shakes her head. "She's not dead, Tim."

Shannon sits beside him at the counter. He wants to apologize to her. But they've had those talks, about his going to Michigan, about her marrying Kevin.

"I went to Michigan because I thought it was the right thing."

"I know, Tim. That was a long time ago." Shannon looks at her pie. "You didn't want to stay, Tim. You didn't want . . . When you went to Michigan, I understood. That maybe you could make it there. Play in the AHL. That we could come and join you. That's what you said. But then when you got sent down—"

"I was going to get sent back up."

"You didn't come home, Tim. Maybe three days at Christmas—"

"I was skating."

"A week in the summer. Presents for Kate, half promises to me. There was nothing solid." She looks at him. "We've had this discussion."

Oak nods. It's true.

"And now this." She looks at him and there's the sadness again in her eyes. "That beautiful face. I remember, when you were fighting in the ring, I didn't want your face to ever get hurt. And even when you were hurting someone else, pounding some poor guy's nose in, I'd remember the sweetness of your face. *I know him*, I'd tell myself, I'd tell anyone who'd listen."

Shannon shakes her head, shaking away her memories. "Kevin read to Kate every night when she was little. When you were wherever you were. When he isn't working, he still meets her at the bus. We go to church, believe it or not. We've been together ten years. Our ten-year anniversary is coming up. He makes the three of us laugh."

Shannon cuts into the pie and he sees her as she was, in a heather sweater, her face flush with cold, doing their homework together. "These pies still suck," Shannon says, and she smiles. She takes a sip of the coffee. She checks her phone. "I have to go, Tim. I'm sorry. The traffic was terrible. I'm meeting Kevin at his mother's."

"How is she?" Oak asks.

Shannon looks at him, shakes her head a little, the smile gone. He's knows he's said the wrong thing. If he wants to know how Slats's mother is, she's just down the road.

"She's fine, Tim." Shannon puts her hat back on. "Kate keeps a picture of you playing hockey on her dresser." She kisses him quickly on the cheek, stands, and goes.

55

Oak blows out cold air. He's got the baggies of heroin inside his shorts. The bar's a new place on Broadway. Barry didn't say anything about a bouncer in a headset. Oak's got Only's gun inside his jacket. If the bouncer moves to frisk him, he'll turn around.

"ID?" the bouncer says.

Oak hands him his ID. The bouncer looks at him, a little too long.

"Everything good?" Oak says, steady, risking a little attitude.

The Bouncer nods. "Texas. I spent time there."

"Where at?"

"Galveston."

"Nice there."

"Not bad." The bouncer hands him back his ID.

Oak pushes through the red velvet curtain.

It's a long, narrow, crowded place, a Puck Fair goat painted above the mirrored bar back, white-framed photos on the wood paneled walls. Hip-hop on the sound system.

Barry said to go to the bar at 7:00 p.m. and order a beer,

drink it, and then go to the men's room and wait. Oak gets to the bar. He waits his turn. There's a woman bartender and a guy with a beard and then he sees a skinny, bald Irish bartender who checks him, he sees it, then goes on pouring Red Bull and vodka into a glass.

The woman comes over. He orders a Bud. Gives her ten. Gets four back, leaves two crossed on the bar. He knows how he looks, gassed, beat-up and nervous, but the place is crowded and the bartenders don't seem to notice or care.

He wants to down the Bud in one. But he sips, trying to figure how much time he should spend drinking it. He's not going to look at the Irish bartender. He sips some more. Two security cameras spin red circles at the ceiling corners of the bar.

He turns and walks through the waiting customers, so there is no doubt about it, so it's clear that he's here and he's intentionally moving, heading to the men's room where Barry said he should just take a piss and wait. Over his shoulder, he sees the Irish barman on his phone.

He shoves the bathroom door open. Barry talked about fingerprints. How you slice the whorl through the first layers of live skin, then fill the cut with crystals of Drano. "Burns you a new ID," his uncle said. "If you can take it."

Inside the men's room are three occupied urinals. Oak waits. Makes like he's checking his phone. One of the urinals comes free. Oak walks slowly to the pisser. He stands there. The guy beside him finishes. The Irish barman comes in as they go out. Oak stares at the wall in front of him. RIP Mikey and the flower syringe. Joan in his arms with her face to his neck, the bird song with her breathing. Kate in the cold on the beach.

The barman gets to the urinal beside him. It's just the two of them now. "Friend of Lauren's?" the barman says, glancing back at the door.

Oak reaches into his pants, gets the baggies.

He turns and walks over to the open toilet stall. He throws them in the toilet.

"Whoa," the bartender says.

Oak flushes the toilet with his boot.

"You're fucked," the bartender says, just as a guy comes in.

Oak wants to pop him. "I know it," Oak says. He shoulders the bartender hard as he passes him and hammers the men's room door, stepping back into the busy bar.

BARRY SWINGS OPEN HIS FRONT DOOR that's hung with a plastic Christmas wreath. He's barefoot in sweats. The apartment reeks of dog and weed. "Tell me the phone call I just got from Patrick was a joke."

Oak stands motionless on Barry's front step.

"You didn't sell it, Tim? You didn't do me?"

"No."

"What the fuck?" Lauren says from somewhere inside.

"SHUT IT."

Niamh starts barking.

Barry steps out onto the icy cement step in his bare feet. He closes the door behind him.

Oak feels the gun in his coat. He remembers the gun Barry keeps by the television.

Barry puts a hand on Oak's shoulder. "You fucking sold it, Tim, didn't you?"

"No."

"You really put it down the toilet?"

"I'll pay you."

"YOU GONNA SHARPEN MY SKATES?" His uncle's voice bounces up the cold street. Then his Uncle is quiet. His uncle looks at him. Barry has tears in his eyes now, his arms have gone slack at his sides. "You're a coward like your father, Tim. Patrick's not your uncle. You're lucky you're going inside."

Barry opens his front door, goes back into his apartment, and slams it shut. The wreath drops to the step. Oak leaves it.

Oak walks down the street, the streetlamps hung with Christmas lights, waiting for a blow to the back that doesn't come.

He walks down to the darkness of the bay. When he can't see any cameras on buildings or lamp posts or trees, he hurls the gun into the black water.

HE GETS TO THE GRAVEYARD where his mother is buried. He stands at her grave. The dirt is frozen mud. He lowers to all fours and sits on the cold grass. Sits there a little longer. Then he gets back up to his feet and goes.

56

Oak drives into Revere. Kate's class, Shannon said, is in an elementary school gym. She gave him the address. Said that's where Kate wanted to meet him after she'd talked to Kate after he'd called. He parks, finds the gym door. Hip-hop pounds through it. He goes inside.

There's maybe a dozen girls dancing on the basketball court, and he's standing there, a few parents over in the bleachers, a few little kids playing by the benches, and there's Kate, in the back of three lines of girls, and she's doing it, she's in black sweats and a white T-shirt, her face is hot and he watches her spinning, throwing her arms up, kicking her leg up into the air and back again behind her. Kate in a photograph, Kate on the mantel, buying her a useless green sweater, Kate studying after school with the special ed tutor, dying her red hair blue, listening to the band on her T-shirt, waiting in the mornings on the bus. Eating dinner with Shannon and Slats. Sleeping at night in her bed. Her black high-tops have neon laces. Whip and Nae Nae, his Florida team used to do it on the bus.

When she turns again she sees him and he sees her happy face go blank. Then she spins away from him and disappears, the music pounding against the hard gym floor, against the bleachers, against his heart and into his head. The music segues and the teacher calls out "free-form," and the girls go crazy, laughing and dancing and the bass rings up his bones and the thick hot air clogs up his lungs. He stands there until he can't stand any longer. He gets himself out of the gym.

He sucks air in the empty school parking lot. Standing beneath the cold high sun, his shadow is a dot on the blacktop. He doesn't have anything to say. It's been too long. He's trying to still his pounding heart.

The gym door opens in a sweep of bass and drums. Kate comes out. She just comes up to him, she's sweating, she's looking at him like he is from some foreign place. Like he's nuts. "Hi, Tim."

"I just wanted to see you," he says.

"I know."

"You were really good."

"I'm in the back."

She looks past him to the road.

"You came to see me," she says.

"Yeah, I did."

She nods, looks back at him. "You look kind of okay." She smiles, her bangs sweating into her eyes. "I got you something," she says.

She reaches into her sweatpants, pulls out a Kleenex. Unwraps it.

It's a green piece of sea glass.

She puts it into his hand. "Your hands are messed up."

"I know."

He sucks snot back up his nose.

"It's because you fight."

She's holding his hand in between hers.

"It's from the beach. Obviously," she says.

He's nodding.

"Okay," she says.

"Okay."

Oak takes off his sweatshirt. "You're gonna be cold."

She puts it on. Two Kates could fit in it.

Cars are pulling into the lot to pick up their daughters.

"You want to go ice skating on the Frog Pond? They got it all done up for Christmas."

"Now?"

"Not now. I mean, soon."

"I know. I was joking." Kate smiles.

"Oh yeah?" Oak smiles. "You're a wise-ass."

"Like you, yeah," she says as behind her the girls flood out of the gym to their parents.

"I got a phone number, you want it?" he says.

"There's Kevin."

Oak sees Slats pulling up in his truck.

"Look. I'm probably going away for six months, I mean to prison. I hit a cop."

"Why?"

"I don't know, Kate. Habit."

"Can I visit?"

Slats is watching them. "Let's go see Kevin."

Oak walks with Kate to the truck. He sees Slats eye his sweatshirt that she's wearing. "I want to give Kate my phone number," Oak says to Slats.

"Does she want it?"

"Yeah," Kate says.

"So give it to her," Slats says.

57

Back at the hospital, there's the black nurse and a white nurse he doesn't recognize.

"There's The Man," the black nurse says, smiling. "They arrested his father."

Oak nods.

"Kip's doing good. Nothing major. Not to his body anyhow."

"I'll go in to see him."

The nurse smiles at him.

The nurse he doesn't know says, "His mother's in there with him."

"That boy doesn't have a mother," he hears the black nurse saying to the new nurse as he heads away down the hall to Kip's room.

When he opens the door, Joan is in the single chair, staring at Kip who is sleeping.

"I should have seen it," Joan says. "His back." She doesn't turn to look at Oak.

"I saw it," Oak says. "I didn't do shit."

"That time when he took Charles's drugs."

He stands beside her. Kip's hooked into an IV. "I threw him out of a car and into a parking lot in Worcester," Oak says watching Kip's hands ball and unball in his sleep. "He was mouthing off. Looking up to me and mouthing off. So I tossed him."

Joan takes Oak's hand.

"You gonna give it up?" Oak says, turning to look at her.

She shrugs. "Are you?"

She hasn't slept either, he can tell. She looks older, her face grayer, her hair falls down into her eyes. "I don't want you to visit when I go away," Oak says. "If you were even thinking of it. I just want to be left alone there."

Joan squeezes his hand. "You don't always get what you want, Tim."

"Hey," Kip wakes up. "Hey—you're here." He says it to Joan.

Joan smiles. "This guy too," she points at Oak.

"Look at my phone," Kip says. "That's what I been meaning to say. Was I saying it?"

Joan gets Kip's phone from his bedside.

"Play the video I shot. It's of him."

Joan turns back to Oak. "Tim?"

"Play it," Oak says.

Joan starts the video on Kip's phone. Oak watches her watch his Worcester collapse.

"Oh, Tim," Joan says, and she takes a sharp inhale of breath. A couple of whistles blow. The video ends. Joan looks at the phone in her hand for a little while.

"What do you think of that?" Kip says.

Joan shakes her head.

"What do *you* think?" Kip says to Oak.

Oak looks at Kip. He says quietly, "I think the guy there had enough."

"Yeah," Kip says, nodding, his face a mess. "Me too."

58

Murphy's Rink is done up for Christmas. At the turnstile, he keeps walking.

"Hey," says the kid behind the counter.

"I'm Tim O'Connor," Oak says. "Ask your father."

Oak changes into his old skates on the benches in front of concessions. No one says anything to him. No one's going to. He gets onto the ice where John and JJ's St. Catherine's team is holding a practice.

He skates out, easy, there with the kids and their parents. He laps the near ice. He laps it again, a little faster. He takes one more lap, harder, and some of the fathers have stopped to watch, he notices, fuck them, let them, he digs in good, and then he finds JJ, standing on the ice with his dad over-coaching him, the two so-called real coaches clustering with the starters while the rest of the players stand ignored to the side.

"Oak."

"John. JJ."

"How you doing?" John says.

They shake.

"Hey JJ—" John calls his son over. JJ skates over. Oak sees the coaches wondering what's up. JJ looks up at Oak from inside his cage. His chubby face is sweating too hard.

"Your coach tells you to shoot from the legs?" Oak asks JJ.

JJ nods.

"Of course," John answers.

"Next time up," Oak says, looking at the coaches, one of whom looks like a Nazi, "shoot from your arms. Forget about your legs. Use your arms and muscle the puck hard into the net."

JJ nods. He skates back to join the line with the other kids.

"Thanks for coming," John says.

Oak has his eyes on the kids.

One kid's a shooter, the rest are St. Catherine mediocre. JJ has no talent. Oak can see it in just the way JJ stands unbalanced on the ice. But JJ's about to put it hard into the net. The coaches aren't even looking, are waiting on the next kid, ignoring JJ and talking to each other. You should never shoot from the arms. But sometimes you should. JJ skates to the blue line. The coach who looks like a fucking Nazi passes JJ the puck and JJ fans, the puck sliding right to where Oak's standing next to JJ's dad at center ice.

"Shit," John says.

"Okay, Bobby—" the coach says to the next kid who's up, JJ slumping toward the goal line for the next drill.

"Again," Oak calls out, his voice big in the live rink air. "JJ, get back to the line."

"Hey, dude—" the coach says.

"JJ," Oak yells out. JJ skates back to the blue line and just as he turns Oak hits him with a kick-pass from his skate before the kid has time to think about it. JJ one-times it, the puck lifting a perfect cold six inches and snapping into the lower right corner of the net.

"And don't forget it," Oak says to JJ, who grins and skates five inches taller to the corner.

"Okay, Bobby," the Nazi coach says, pissed.

"That's Tim O'Conner," John announces to the team and the other coach nods his head, impressed even.

"No shit?" the other coach says, and they're all looking at him now.

He'll talk to Arlene. He'll ask her to help him set up accounts for Kate and for Kip from the money he's going to get from the sale of the house. For dance lessons and college. For piano lessons and college. He's worked it out in his head.

"Oak, Oak, Oak!" a kid suddenly starts chanting and then all the kids are chanting, like they even know who the fuck he is. He feels John slap him on the back. The coach who he guesses knows who he is skates over with his stick.

"Will you take a few shots, Tim, you know, for the kids?" the coach says.

Oak takes the stick. Flexes and balls his hands.

The kids stand there. A couple of them skate to the boards for their parents to give them their phones. Like something's going to happen.

It is.

Oak skates to the blue line. "Okay, Coach," he says to the dick, who lays a pass at him so slack that Oak misses it by a good eight inches. A couple kids laugh.

Oak feels it in him, rising. He looks back at the coach. "Pass the fucking puck, man, I'm not twelve years old."

The coach snaps one at him. Oak lays it hard and fast into the upper left corner of the net.

"Come on," Oak says. "Harder—"

He ropes it into the upper right.

"Harder—"

The coach slaps at him from the corner, Oak spinning, catching the puck with his leg, the puck dropping straight down, Oak timing the small, flat bounce and drilling it into the back of the net, the cheap goal bursting from its mooring, Oak seeing Plymouth Prison clear, cold on a brilliant winter's day.

ACKNOWLEDGMENTS

This book would not have been completed without the help of Noah Ballard, Meagan Brothers, Scott Cheshire, Amey Miller, Brian Sides, Michael Signorelli, and Vikki Warner. Thank you.

And thank you, Zena Coffman, Deirdre Curley, Holly Frederick, Lauren Maturo, Hannah Ohlmann, Josie Woodbridge, and everyone on the Blackstone Publishing and Curtis Brown teams.

For encouragement and support across the writing of this book, thank you, Chad Benton, Carol Chu, Hyland Harris, John Van Wettering and all at CK Chu Tai Chi, Katherine Holmes-Chuba and Dan, Nick and Olivia Chuba, Menna Elfyn, David Burr Gerrard, David Gordon Green, Mark Halliday and Jill Rosser, Ken Hart, Dwight and Mindy Hilson, Gerry Holmes, Julia Holmes, Kris Jansma, Paul Levitz, Susan Lilly, Steve Montal, Lisa Muskat, Jeff Pearlman, Bernard and Catherine Plansky, John Proctor and Christine Dehne, Max Schott, Jonathan Tropper, Tyler Wetherall. Thank you to Manhattanville College. And thank you to my colleagues in the English department, Caralyn Bialo, Meghan Freeman, Nada Halloway, Van Hartmann, David

Lugowski, Mark Nowak, Lori Soderlind. And to the creative writing team at the Dowd-O'Gorman Center for Creative Writing, including Sharbari Ahmed, Bryce Bauer, Shane Cashman, Sally Bliumis-Dunn, Mark Lungariello, and the many others who have taught with us over the years. Thanks to my students who are often also my teachers. Thank you to Martha and Carey and Lucy and Karl for always opening their homes for laughs and conversation. Thank you to Eric for still being willing to talk sports in this age of corporate boxes.

And thank you to Meagan who inspires me with her beautiful work and beautiful self.